Endorsements for Grayson's Legacy

"Grayson's Legacy" captivated me from the outset. It was like reading a mystery thriller. Upon completion I read it again and again and again. Into this intriguing novel, Murray has masterfully woven an important message, yet in a most natural way. It reveals matters we are all aware of, even struggle with, and yet lack understanding of or a solution for. This book provides the solution. Get ready for your heart to be profoundly touched, your emotions deeply stirred and very possibly—some tears to flow. It will become a best-seller.

(Graham Powell, Pastor, Teacher, Author,
Qualicum Beach, B.C., Canada.)

"Grayson's Legacy" captured my imagination early on for a number of reasons, but primarily because I found myself in the story! My forebears took the same journey from England some 20 years later than Grayson; I have also relocated my family to Christchurch making this our home so found the historical accounts both fascinating as well as historically accurate. But perhaps most of all I resonated with the 'beneath the surface' issues that plagued Grayson and his family line. It became my story, my wrestling for wholeness, my desire to unlock this glorious love of God that leaves a healthy inheritance for the generations to follow.

With the challenges that we have faced recently in Christchurch with severe earthquakes and the resulting destruction, hearing the wonderful stories of the foundations of the city recorded in "Grayson's Legacy" encouraged me to embrace the future with a renewed enthusiasm. Perhaps 'listening and learning' from our past and understanding how it shapes our current reality is one of the greatest legacy's we can leave the following generations. I encourage you to read this enthralling story, to listen to your own story and allow your future to be unlocked in ways that leave a legacy of abundance and opportunity.

(Donald Scott, Senior Pastor, North City Church, Christchurch, NZ
Communication & Leadership Strategist)

An intriguing mystery. A compelling journey. A great rea

(Fraser Hardy, Leader of the
of Ch

"I enjoyed reading Murray's book "Grayson's Legacy." It was hard to put down as I laughed and cried through the chapters. This book provides interesting insights that will be helpful for anyone and it offers an understanding of truth that could well serve the increasing numbers of despondent and dysfunctional people in the here and now. I found it quite emotional as one of my great-grandfathers was shipped out to New Zealand at the age of seventeen in similar circumstances to "Grayson."

(Hudson Salisbury,
Pioneering NZ Church Leader and Elder Statesman)

"The history of Christchurch and Canterbury came alive for me as I read "Grayson's Legacy," reminding me of the youth of New Zealand as a nation and the remarkable decision that its first European settlers made in traveling to its shores."

(Steve Howse,
General Manager, Award Winning NZ Business Leader)

In "Grayson's Legacy," Murray has given his readers a clearer understanding of the consequences of how one's actions can impact us and our children's children—the nature of generational curses. It is also an interesting read relative to the early history of New Zealand. Get ready to consider your ways.

(Timothy M. Gustafson, Counsellor, Life Consultant,
Author of "The ABC's of Marriage," Overland Park, Kansas, US)

Nobody will be able to finish reading "Grayson's Legacy" without being deeply moved by a historical story of dysfunction, brokenness, and ultimately, redemption. With its underlying message of how a father's choices impact his family, it will undoubtedly stir a fresh desire in the reader to truly connect with their own family and invite God's grace and restoration into every area of their lives.

(Christina Simmonds, Health Professional, Community/
Humanitarian Aid worker)

GRAYSON'S LEGACY

"It is easier to build strong children than to repair broken men."
Frederick Douglass

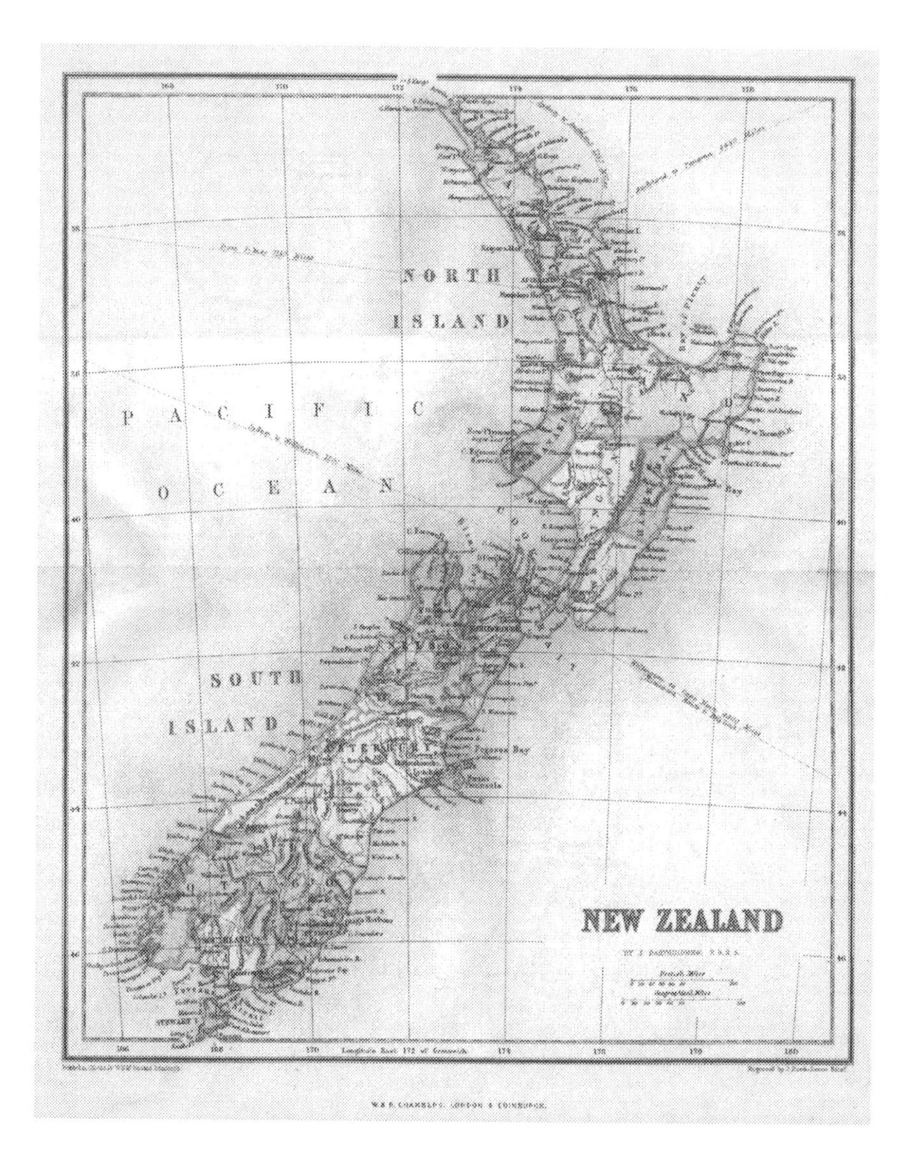

Authentic Cartography 1846 New Zealand.
Used by permission www.hipkiss.org/data/maps/nz

GRAYSON'S LEGACY

A father's dark secrets leave his son a shocking inheritance

An historical novel by

MURRAY R.N. SMITH

All of the characters portrayed in this story are represented as creations of the author's imagination. They are not intended to resemble anyone in real life by name or any other likeness; such similarity must be deemed to be entirely coincidental.

Painting on front dust jacket flap of the hardcover version used by permission of the National Maritime Museum in Greenwich, London.

WestBow Press books may be ordered through booksellers or by contacting:

WestBow Press
A Division of Thomas Nelson
1663 Liberty Drive
Bloomington, IN 47403
www.westbowpress.com
1-(866) 928-1240

ISBN: 978-1-4497-9054-7 (sc)
ISBN: 978-1-4497-9056-1 (hc)
ISBN: 978-1-4497-9053-0 (e)

Library of Congress Control Number: 2013907492

Scripture taken from the King James Version of the Bible.

Printed in the United States of America.

WestBow Press rev. date: 05/03/2013

For the brave people of Christchurch, New Zealand who have suffered extremely in earthquakes over recent years, particularly the February 2011 quake which claimed the lives of 185 people and caused widespread destruction and damage.

The courage and resilience of these people as they de-construct and rebuild their broken city reflects the same pioneering spirit of the original settlers whose vision in first establishing Christchurch, meant that there would even *be* a future and a story to tell.

A special thanks to my beautiful, gifted wife Michelle, my family and Bridges Church, Cambridge, New Zealand who have provided a safe place to dream, to serve and to create.

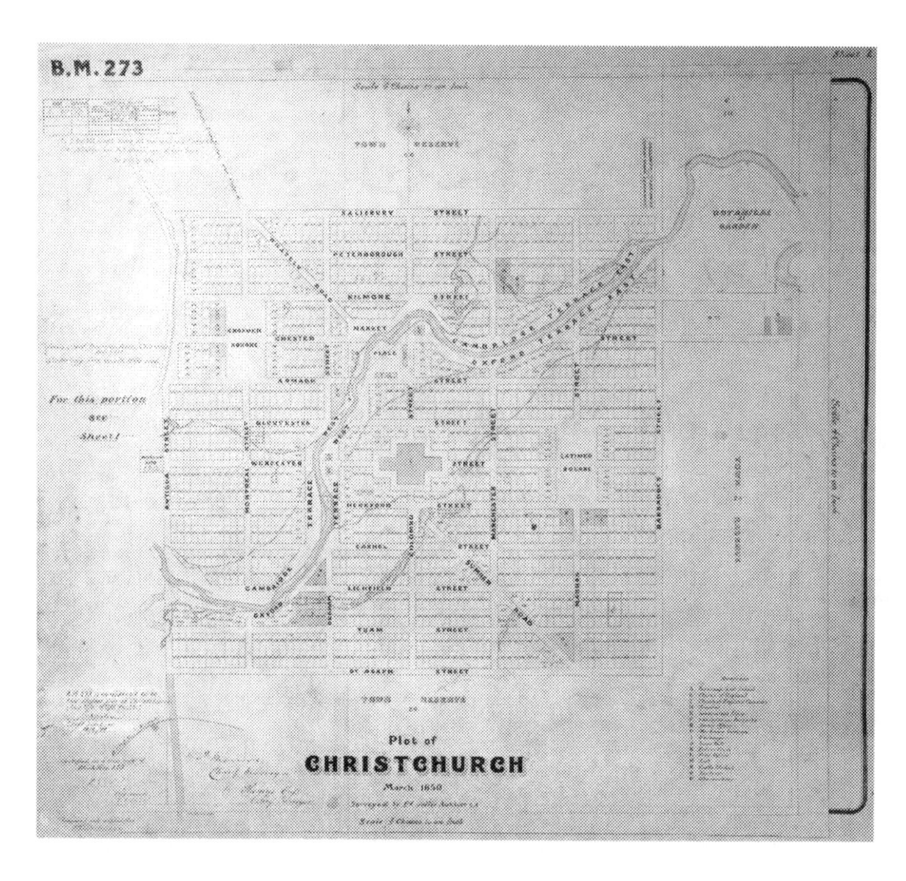

1850 Survey Plan City of Christchurch, New Zealand
Used by permission of Archives New Zealand Christchurch Office
The Department of Internal Affairs Te Tari Taiwhenua

TABLE OF CONTENTS

PREFACE

This is an historical novel based solidly on facts surrounding a fascinating era in the history of New Zealand from the 1850's and onwards. A young boy out of a broken family situation is sent away from his home in England, leaving everything that was familiar to him and made to be a part of British colonial expansion into the Canterbury region of New Zealand. The story records how this rejected and wounded boy's life unfolds. It provides moving and telling insight into the nature of how human failings and brokenness, have the ability to create an impact that travels progressively down through a family generational line.

"Grayson's Legacy" opens up the possibility that deep negative issues lingering in the *past* of a family lineage, can, and may well need to be resolved in the *present.*

This narrative will stir fathers in particular, to rise to the privilege of raising their families in such a way that they leave behind them a positive inheritance for successive generations to walk in.

1

A FAMILY IN PAIN

Grayson Pollock was an appealing, winsome child, but it seemed there always had been a certain withdrawn sadness about him. Large, doleful grey-blue eyes set deeply in pale cheeks stared out from behind his long, dark lashes. Grayson was of average height for his age, and his slender frame and stooping posture somehow assisted an impression that he was cowering.

Others usually assumed that his introversion was merely a feature of temperament, and it became accepted that Grayson was just a very inward child. Examination as to whether there might be possible underlying causes for the traits he manifested were apparently overlooked or had been put aside. Such trivialization left Grayson identified as merely being an introverted little personality with scarcely any thought ever given to a possible connection between his upbringing and his disposition.

At some level, in the heart of every little boy resides the longing to feel he is special. Grayson was no exception, and that longing was most keenly felt in relation to his father, a man who displayed profound ineptitude at nurturing his son's feelings of belonging and being wanted.

Some little boys grow up fatherless through a tragedy that physically separates father from son. Perhaps a far greater tragedy though, is for a son to grow up not fatherless in the sense of having lost a father, but having a father who is there yet somehow *absent* for any number of reasons. Such a father, through his disengagement, falls from the task and privilege of being there in a way that ultimately will provide his son with essential preparation for life.

For the males of the Pollock family, it seemed for generations that an undefinable lack of connection existed between fathers and sons. Manifesting in a variety of ways in this family, the evidence of fundamental difficulty repetitively surfaced. Whether it was a kind of stoicism or a stiff upper lip syndrome in the males, it seemed just too uncomfortable to ever talk about feelings or to candidly share on matters of the heart. To ever indulge in open, heartfelt reality in conversation was deemed to exhibit weakness.

Such dysfunction had taken its toll in the life of little Grayson James Pollock. Possessed of the natural yearning any young son has for a father's affirmation and attention, he grew up through early childhood years under the sterile regimen of a father who provided adequately at a practical level yet neglected any emotional nurture. His father was either unaware or incapable of arresting any internal deficit accruing in his son as he grew up with a quiet desperation for the slenderest inkling of his father's approval.

The manner in which it was confirmed to Grayson beyond any doubt that he could not be that special to his papa was both shocking and scandalous in 1850. It began with being called in to the front room to have a "little talk" on that horrible, blustery September day in London, England. By the time the meeting was over, a total sense of isolation and abandonment was thoroughly imparted to Grayson, and rejection and insecurity as well.

It wasn't that he *was* unloved by his father; it just was never expressed in ways that made it clear to Grayson that he carried much value or significance. Even though he dared to hope and longed for this to be the case, the affirmation he courted and sought was never received, leaving Grayson wrestling with a deep sense of being a bothersome nuisance of little consequence and forever feeling in the way.

At least that was how it appeared in the mind of this nine-year-old. The meeting he was about to be brought into would do nothing to allay any of those feelings. In fact, the realities about to be disclosed would explode in this young life in such a way that the course of his future would be shatteringly altered. What he was about to discover about some of his father's choices and the resultant outflow of shame and knee-jerk response held the potential to fortify every one of those lurking feelings of insignificance, and it would mark the course of his life.

Grayson had always been aware that there was a certain silence surrounding his father's background. Family matters were not spoken of openly, and it never seemed welcoming territory for a small boy growing up to delve into such areas.

Timidly making his way along the dark hallway and approaching the heavy, stained oak panel door of the front room, Grayson wondered what this summons could be about. Such visits were normally reserved for occasions when warnings or discipline awaited. He couldn't recollect anything he might have done to warrant this visit.

Heart pounding, he knocked and pushed the heavy door open upon hearing a muffled voice he did not immediately recognize extend the invitation to come in.

Grayson's mother sat in the window seat, slightly silhouetted. Her head was bowed, and without altering her downward gaze to look at Grayson, she extended her hand toward him. Nervously Grayson shuffled his way to her, eyes searching her face for understanding as to what might be happening. Her unusually pale complexion and swollen, red-rimmed eyes that had emptied themselves of tears were clear enough evidence of some inner turmoil she was enduring. Staring up into her face trying to catch her eye, Grayson caught her bottom lip lightly trembling.

He had seen his mother upset many times in the past, but the child sensed that this occasion was somehow more potent than anything he had ever observed previously. The atmosphere of the room was charged in a way that even a young boy could not miss.

There were two other shadowy figures in the room, which Grayson initially took little notice of while being aware of their presence. One was his grandfather, and Grayson fleetingly thought the other with his back turned was his father. He shot a nervous glance in the man's direction, and while noting he was a similar build to his father, he looked somewhat fresher and perhaps a little younger. Grayson did not recall ever having seen this person before.

Where was his father?

After sniffing into the air and then clearing his throat with a rather labored rattle, Grandfather spoke bluntly and formally, with his usual lack of warmth.

"Grayson, we need to inform you of something," he said quietly. "However, first, an introduction. Grayson, this is Mr. Sutcliffe."

The other man in the room stepped forward and took Grayson's hand. "Pleased to meet you, son. You can call me Tom. Looking forward to getting to know you."

As the stranger stepped back, Grayson eyed him cautiously, wondering what the proposal of "getting to know you" was about. A sense of mild resistance to what was starting to feel like an ambush arose in Grayson.

"Grayson, you won't be seeing your father again, I'm afraid," continued Grandfather, "something all of us would be the better for, if it could be managed." His voice was taut with anger.

Unable to comprehend the words and the dynamic he was being thrust into, yet knowing it was serious, Grayson opened his mouth to say something, but words wouldn't come. His mind struggled. *Not seeing father again? Why? Is he dead? What has happened? Can someone please make this clear?*

Grayson glanced at his mother, who remained statuesque at the window box seat, refusing to catch his or anyone else's eye. She was clearly caught up in dealing with what was unfolding herself. For a little boy with insecurities already formulated to a high level, this inexplicable and bewildering conversation set his young mind racing.

"Whhy?" A pathetic little croak emerged from Grayson's tightening throat as he fought back the urge to burst into tears.

"Your father has bought shame upon our whole family, and this includes you," Grandfather bristled.

"Where is he?" asked Grayson, finding both his voice and courage.

"In another part of London, where he will be staying," said Grandfather. Then, turning slightly in the stranger's direction, he muttered quiet words that would have meant little to Grayson even if he had caught them. *"With that creature and their illegitimate children."*

"I should like to see my Papa and talk to him," said Grayson, sensing the disapproval even as he raised the prospect. "When will he be coming home?"

"Your father will not be seeing you. And this certainly is no longer his home. He will not be so much as entering. There is nothing further to be said on the subject," retorted Grandfather.

"But I must see my papa," protested the child feebly. Tears were now flowing as this little boy realized he was just a bit player in a script that had already been written by adult determinations, which he was powerless to have any influence in.

"But Mama, tell them. Tell Grandfather that I *will* be seeing Papa. You could take me to him now, couldn't you?"

His mother inched her face a fraction toward him, darted a furtive glance his way and whispered in a hushed voice, "No, I'm afraid I shan't be taking you near your father. He has another life that has no room for you or for me."

"But I must be with him…and he *wants* me."

They were desperately hopeful words that lacked inner assurance even as Grayson forlornly mouthed them. Inside, confused emotions tumbled in chaotic fashion as he struggled to grasp what was being expressed as his entire world threatened to crumble. His life, with its hopes and dreams, was being dismantled by agendas he was powerless to influence.

Unanswered questions scrolled rapidly in his mind like passing movie credits. *No more Father? Even though he is somewhere else, he cannot see me. Does he want to see me? Have I been such a very bad boy he does not want me? Is he sad about what is happening? How can I fix this? What will happen to me?*

A sense of hot, frightened anger rose up from somewhere inside, and he shouted, "You all know nothing—*nothing.* You hate me, and Papa loves me! You're all mean and horrible! You can't stop me from being with him and talking to him!"

The firm hands of Mr. Sutcliffe grabbing Grayson's shoulders as he started a futile dash for the door, contrasted with this stranger's gentle tone of voice.

"Your father cares for you and hopes one day you will understand. But for now he is busy with another family where he is their papa too."

For Grayson the implications of others calling his father 'papa' were too complex to even start to get a grip on. Even for an adult it was difficult to understand the strange story that had only recently been uncovered of how a man could fragment himself to the point of having two wives and two separate families residing in the same city each oblivious of the other's existence. What impossible agonies of inner turmoil would a man have to be possessed of to make choices over time that would lead to such a predicament? Such duplicity could scarcely be imagined.

"I am going to go with you on an adventure on a beautiful big ship. Together you and I will sail the oceans to another place. We will travel and see exciting things and discover another life."

Mr. Sutcliffe's staggering announcement was delivered in an effort to be positive but somehow it sounded hollow and hardly enough to even slightly distract Grayson from the shock and confusion his mind was reeling under.

But there it was. Tom Sutcliffe had indeed been given custodial guardianship of nine-year-old Grayson James Pollock. Already passage for two had been paid in full to sail away from Plymouth in four days time—away from home and everything familiar.

Many would see it as a bizarre, misguided plan formulated perhaps out of the irrationality of shock and grief as a coping mechanism. How the plan might have offered a solution or heal the heartrending emotions of pain and grief that were being experienced, is unclear. How a mother and grandfather could accede to such a course of action, believing it was for the child's best, would to many, be unfathomable.

But it was their plan, and it had been decided to be for the best, as they saw it. In time, the decision would prove to further consolidate a family dynamic that was emerging and becoming entrenched as an integral part of the Pollock family "inheritance" for generations to come.

2

THE LEAVING

Sleep did not come easily to Grayson as he tossed and turned restlessly in bed that night thinking about his father. There was so little he really knew or understood about him. A child of his age could never take into account the factors that had contributed to the paternal neglect he had suffered as a result of the brokenness in his father's experience of life.

Although the understanding Grayson had of his father's upbringing was very sketchy, he had gained sufficient information to have put the basics together that his papa's life had not been easy.

Grayson's father had been raised initially by his grief stricken mother—a woman whose husband had chosen to forsake his marriage and infant son to live abroad. The abandoned little boy had grown up with only fleeting recollections from earliest childhood of ever having had a dad. In that day and age, precious little help was available for a mother and a young child in such a predicament, unless it was provided for by caring family members. As a fatherless child—Grayson's dad was cared for by his mother, a woman whose sorrow apparently never relented after being abandoned. She struggled to make life work at any level and after several years, upon her death, the child was received into the home of extended family members on the mother's side. This little Pollock boy had then grown up withdrawn and exhibiting significant identity issues. While not lacking in suitable material provision, it was clear that any lack lay in the influence of a real father's nurturing love and attention.

So it was, Grayson's father had grown into young manhood in an environment where he had been adopted under a certain sense of obligation. His early experience of family was stilted and joyless with scant demonstration of basic roles and essentially no opportunity for learning or gaining relational skills and aptitude.

Full of false expectations of what having a wife might accomplish in his life and eager to find love and affirmation, Grayson's father had found himself unprepared in every respect for a marriage that was formed in rather unnatural circumstances. He had married the daughter of his adoptive parents after a covert courtship. This girl who would become Grayson's mother had resisted her father's strong disapproval of the union stemming from his concern that the young man who sought his daughter's hand had issues that could surface and that all did not bode well for a happy marriage. Sadly the misgivings of her father proved accurate with the brokenness and lack in the new groom multiplying in the marriage until it became a routine disappointment—full of lost expectation and broken dreams…a relationship where joyful sharing and communication might have flourished instead had been diminished to the level of dutiful survival.

It wasn't ugly. It was just far below what both husband and wife somehow sensed might be attainable with the expectations they sought of one another elusively escaping them. They were two hearts bound in matrimony but missing the point and continually "missing" each other. They shared little connection—sadly their story was all too common in that day. This was an era for the most part, when many loveless marriages dutifully endured under the pressure of social norms with little or no assistance to support the recovery or revitalizing of a failing relationship.

As a grey dawn broke, Grayson struggled groggily out of broken fitful sleep.

The old clock on the mantle in the kitchen chimed as daylight struggled in through the net curtaining that hung over the large sash window above the sink. The smell of the wood burning stove drifted through the hallway down into Grayson's little room. This was a household that had been up since well before dawn.

It was 6.15 am on the 7th day of September 1850…a day he held little sense of excitement for. In fact he had gone to bed the last few nights lying there hoping that he was in a very strange dream out of which he would awake and find everything was normal again.

This morning heralded his last chance to savor the familiarity of his mother and father's sparse little cottage where had had lived since he was born on the 17th day of December 1840.

Grayson had not seen his father for over a week now and was still coming to grips with the announcement that had come like a double-edged sword—firstly that he would *never* see his father again, secondly that he would be deported to New Zealand supposedly for his protection and the "realizing of his potential in an untainted environment". That was the rhetoric, whatever it was supposed to mean.

This was a time when emigration to the new colonies was becoming a serious consideration for some, but for a boy not yet ten years old, it was a terrifying edict. Grayson had pleaded before an unrelenting grandfather and a mother, who for all intents and purposes had completely shut down and proved to be incapable of any rational entreaty.

A few days earlier he had learned his father was a "bigamist"… a term he had now heard adults use a few times but didn't have much of a clue what it meant. All he understood was that his father was husband to another woman with another family and that from now on, in their view, this meant there was no room for Grayson and his mother. What was unclear was whether his father agreed with that stance or had much knowledge of the proceedings that had been instigated. Certainly there was no opportunity extended for this father who could not possibly have imagined that he would never be seeing his son again, to express anything. His feelings and opinions did not even count as it had been deemed by Grayson's grandfather that the man's failures earned him forfeiture of viewpoint or access. All of this was a consequence of his mysterious duplicitous lifestyle that had dramatically unfolded in the past several weeks. What seemed very clear was that at no point in the future would opportunity ever be extended to this father for contact if it could be helped.

Grayson pulled the bed covers over his head at the sound of approaching footsteps. If it was his grandfather, he wanted to make himself scarce. Grandfather had taken over everything and it now seemed somehow to Grayson that even his presence bothered the old man to the point of provoking him to seething irritation. Perhaps the boy was a symbol and a reminder to the old man of the injury that had been already done to his daughter who he was now anxious to shield from further pain.

But oddly enough it was the pain of a nine-year-old boy that appeared to be disregarded. Although he had no vocabulary for it, Grayson felt a deep sense of shame inside for which he could not give an account. It just sat there hanging over him like an accusation that would not lift off.

"Time to get up," Grandfather said gruffly with a measure of severity that let Grayson know that this was final and not to be trifled with. Being stern was something this grandfather had made an art form of over the years, but this was even more abrupt than usual.

"Mr. Sutcliffe is here and soon it will be time to leave." His voice trailed off as he stepped out of the doorway and walked back down the hallway.

Grayson pulled himself up and sat on the edge of the bed eyeing his surroundings. Aware he was taking in one last look at the little room where he had made his hideaway since infancy, he felt a strange pang of isolation. If this would not be his place anymore where might it be in the future? A little shudder went through his slight frame as a cold sense of uncertainty flooded over him.

At the foot of the bed lay a little pile of clothes his mother had laid out neatly for him the day before with a small, weather-beaten, brown leather suitcase which contained everything in this world, other than memories, that one small boy would take to the other side of the world. Buttoning up his shirt, the lump he had felt in his throat since the front room meeting seemed more intense than ever.

Tears misted his eyes as he tied his bootlaces. He remembered the moment so long ago of how proud he'd been when, for the first time, he had shown his father that he had finally mastered the task unassisted.

Grayson's mother glided into the room and sat on the bed silently…not that she was anything more than silent most of the time. He felt quite sure that she loved him but had always longed to hear the words spoken and craved for her embrace that would assure him that she cared. Locked up in her own struggles she appeared incapable of meaningful verbal or physical expression. In early childhood Grayson had vivid memories of his father on a couple of occasions attempting to show a little tender physical affection and the small boy had delighted in the prospect of seeing his mother responding warmly. It had pained him to see his father brushed off and Grayson sensed the lack of closeness this behavior perpetuated.

Even now at such a time, when with such finality she was about to say goodbye, her eyes flickered nervously, darting around the room, refusing to rest on her only son for too long. Maybe it was her strategy of self-protection, but in years to come Grayson would frequently ponder this stilted moment when his mother had an opportunity to say things he so wanted to hear, but she couldn't say them. Surely now was the chance to effusively demonstrate how this situation was one which she didn't really want and to state how it broke her heart. To hear her say that she would miss him every minute of every day would have meant everything. Yet the little photograph Grayson had of her packed in his suitcase, exhibited as much emotion as his mother herself in those moments.

Sutcliffe came into the room and stood there awkwardly. It was clear that here was a decent sort of man who was somehow caught up in fulfilling a role he did not relish as a service to Grayson's grandfather.

"There's toast and tea in the kitchen," Sutcliffe said softly while Grayson's mother slipped past him and down the hallway.

"The coach for Paddington will be here in a few minutes."

Grayson had no appetite but sipped the lukewarm cup of sweetened tea.

Soon a knock on the door heralded the arrival of the coach. Grandfather opened the door and a short plump man doffed his cap in greeting. Wordlessly, Grandfather with the little brown leather suitcase in hand, led the way out into the crisp morning, down the front steps to the waiting coach. The blinkered horse snorted bursts of steamy vapor from her nostrils into the cold atmosphere. Sutcliffe jumped in the side door first and Grayson scrambled in after him. The coachman closed the door while the little boy stared back out the window to see his grandfather on the cobbled sidewalk with one hand raised bidding farewell, the other tucked into his waistcoat pocket. Inside the house he saw his mother at the bay window holding back the curtain, waving with a little handkerchief in her hand. She was sobbing.

And then with a lurch they were off. Just like that.

Long gone now was the wishing that this was an unpleasant dream. For Grayson it was now all too real. They were on their way to catch the train from Paddington Station to Plymouth where a ship would set sail the next day. And he would be on that ship bound for a country halfway around the world that he knew nothing about with a man looking after him whom he barely knew. Tom Sutcliffe was likeable enough with a kind manner and warm heart. He seemed to know intuitively how Grayson felt about things in the times they'd spent together in the last few days and was usually prepared to listen if Grayson tried to express something. This had all happened so fast and Tom appreciated that fact, accurately sensing the impact it would have had on the boy's psyche.

He loosened his necktie and looked down at his small charge. Here was a boy whose life had suddenly become like a cork tossed on a tempestuous sea. Tom felt deeply for the anguish this little fellow must surely be feeling. He did not want any complicity in adding pain to this already damaged life and secretly would have preferred not to have the guardianship role that had been thrust upon him. Once it had been discovered that he was making a second trip to New Zealand, a place where he was well connected and had advocated for as a young vibrant colony with exciting opportunities, it had been seized upon by Grayson's grandfather as a solution to the humiliating difficulties he perceived would plague their family. Trying to cope with the judgmental norms of a disapproving nineteenth century mindset was a prospect the grandfather could not face. Besides, he was ageing, his daughter was in no fit state to mother her child and Tom Sutcliffe owed him a considerable favor. It might not be a perfect solution but it was the best he could concoct and manipulate into being.

The coach trip to Paddington Station took twenty minutes. Alighting at the station the duo grabbed their bags, surprised to find even at this time of the morning, a noisy bustling hive of activity. This was a time when the technologies of the day were in a highly accelerated mode, particularly as it related to transport and communication. The new techniques of mass production and precision engineering had re-invented time and opened up a plethora of new opportunity. Railway had in a remarkable way, imposed a transformation upon society all of it's own…timetabled, regulated, precise.

Tom Sutcliffe and Grayson had barely got themselves on the right platform and clambered on board a carriage behind the giant huffing puffing steam locomotive bound for Plymouth when the clock on the central tower struck 7.00am and started clanging out a repetitive reveille.

The piercing shrill of the steam engine's whistle cut through the din and with much hissing and roaring the train shook itself into life and unleashed its momentum as with increasing pace it began pulling away from the platform.

Grayson, face pressed to the window, leaving behind all that had been familiar to him, felt disenfranchised and vulnerable.

As the locomotive made its way through the railway network that threaded across London, it was not long before first the urban and then the industrial vista began to give way to a more rural scene.

"Why did you say to Grandpa that you would take me with you?" asked Grayson. This was hardly a random question but one which he had pondered deeply.

"Well he asked me to," said Tom running his hand down his heavy moustache and stroking his chin anticipating where this line of questioning would head.

"Do you like him?" persisted the boy.

"He has some good qualities to be certain," Sutcliffe responded evasively.

"But how did he make you take me with you?" Grayson probed.

"It wasn't like he *made* me but I was obliged to your Grandfather and he believed that it was best for your future to leave London and for..." his voice trailed off as Grayson interrupted.

"Do you think it's best for me to leave because it is very frightening and won't I miss my home very much?" he asked, his voice quivering as images of his father's and mother's faces flashed through his mind. Something he'd tried to avoid happening.

"I can't say."

"But," he continued, "I've promised your Grandpa and I promise *you* that I'll do my very best to look after you. I'm not your Papa and I've never been a Papa but I think I know how to take care of a young fellow such as yourself."

Grayson was still not satisfied and had to figure out the reason that a virtual stranger could be compelled to take someone else's child away like this.

"Why can Grandpa *make* you take me though?"

"Like I said, he didn't make me but it is true that I owe him a lot. One day I'll explain this to you, but for now *please* know I'm *not* taking you because I *have* to...I've agreed to take you because I like you a lot."

Tom had taken Grayson's hand and held it gently as he spoke. Sensing him recoil just ever so slightly, Tom let the boy's hand go and then silence descended for what seemed ages but was in reality only a few minutes.

Grayson looked at Tom, searching his face for any clue as to how genuine what he had just heard might be. He was looking for ulterior motive, since he was utterly unaccustomed to being told such a thing and didn't know how to respond. Those words. To be told someone *liked* him was something Grayson would savor and live on the strength of for a long time. But he was wary.

"So then it's because you're sorry for me?"

"Well...yes, I, I mean noo...well, sort of. It's just that I think you deserve a shot at a good life and I couldn't see how that might happen for you in England."

Grayson slumped back into his seat, retreating, silent now with his own thoughts until he drifted off into a restless emotionally exhausted sleep.

Off the hook for the moment, Tom looked down at this little boy. Under a cloth cap, his lightly freckled little face was etched with worry lines that reflected concerns and burdens beyond his tender years. Behind those dark eyes brooded all manner of doubts about his value and worth. Poor little chap. He was a helpless little figure really. What would his life become?

Tom felt scared too but would never admit it to Grayson. Of course it would have been much easier doing this trip alone and charting a direction for his own life without this sad little straggler alongside. Hearing the words come from his own mouth, *"I like you a lot,"* had been a bit of a surprise to him. He did like this little boy and felt deeply sorry that in a sense, he was being cast off.

It seemed nobody felt responsible enough to take him and shield him from the mess his family had become.

Sitting there, Tom remembered an old saying, *"The child is father to the man".*

He couldn't recall where he had heard this but it struck him as a profound saying as he thought about it. He contemplated all the many ways that the rubbish of life, just from existing as a human being, can be deposited in a person in such a way that it puts a warp on their soul and personality. He wasn't judging Grayson's father—rather, from what he knew of the man's upbringing, Tom could see how as a *"victim"* the father had himself perhaps unknowingly become a *perpetrator* of some kind of "flow down" effect that was now impacting upon little Grayson.

This little dozing boy he now gazed at would grow into manhood and in all likelihood, be a father to a son one day himself.

'The child is father to the man...'

Tom wondered what the chances were that any son of Grayson's might ever have of experiencing some kind of *normal* family life; could it be reasonable to expect such a boy to emerge from childhood into functional manhood considering the events of recent days together with everything else he knew already of the brokenness in the Pollock line...?

Tom mused on how it felt like he was witnessing legacy in the making as it was being passed onto Grayson James Pollock. The question uppermost in his mind was *what legacy might Grayson James Pollock be in turn, capable of passing on to his offspring?*

3

SAILING THE HIGH SEAS

The **Sir George Seymour** weighed anchor at Plymouth Harbour about midday on Sunday September 8th 1850. She was a full rigged ship; a three masted square rig, 850 tons with 40 cabin, 23 intermediate and 164 steerage passengers. The ship was in the capable and experienced hands of a Captain Goodson who had sailed from England to the new colony of Canterbury in New Zealand previously.

There was no talkative humor when the emigrants had boarded the ship as for most, to quote one passenger, *"they took a last long aching gaze at their native shore."* However, despite the subdued tone of the departure, there was hope for a good future and this balmed the palpable sense of uncertainty that hung in the air.

Tom Sutcliffe and young Grayson Pollock had found their cramped little quarters among the steerage passengers and stowed their bags. Tom actually had a wooden sea chest with a large lock on the lid just below some large initials, *"TPS",* which had been carved ornately into the timber.

Grayson's little brown leather suitcase and its contents was all that he had of this world's goods apart from what he stood up in… the suitcase contained a few clothes, a spare pair of shoes, a warm oilskin coat and three or four photos.

But now there had also been added, a mysterious late addition to the suitcase.

Tom had given this to him when they had arrived dockside at Plymouth. It was a small, blackish brown leather bound book that Grayson's grandfather had apparently instructed Tom to give Grayson at an opportune moment. It looked like a journal kept by Grayson's father, which the grandfather had grudgingly agreed could be passed onto the boy. His mother had apparently overcome her father's resistance to the notion that Grayson should be allowed to have some small reminder of his father. He'd quickly recognized the neat cursive handwriting as that of his father but strangely he felt an aversion to reading it…at least for now anyway. He had flicked through its pages and put it into the bottom of his suitcase for some other time. Its contents could potentially delight him or destroy him. Grayson wasn't ready to take the chance on the latter happening.

Maybe he'd look at it over the next three months or so when this ship would be their "home".

Compared with the privileges cabin passengers enjoyed of more space, privacy and better food, between the decks below, the steerage passengers experienced conditions that were confined and unpleasant. Here, they slept in tiers of bunks and were supplied with mattresses but no bedding. Tom had installed a little hammock arrangement for Grayson who seemed to have a great need for visual contact with his guardian in spite of the close proximity such cramped conditions naturally provided.

Three compartments made up the steerage passenger areas: single men occupying the forward section next to the crew's quarters; single women were aft; and married couples were in the middle.

While each passenger would have their own individual motivations and reasons for embarking on such a voyage, at the time, these travellers were virtually afforded pilgrim status by the populace of the day. The colonist spirit of resolution was strong and hope prophesied better things beyond, which helped passengers endure the discomforts of confinement, extreme heat, extreme cold, sickness, not to mention the presence of danger at sea.

These passengers would certainly endure their share of discomfort but for the present, the ship made an excellent run out of channel and by the 13th was abreast of Cape Finisterre. On Sunday the 15th, the passengers assembled for the first time for divine worship that was held on the *poop* deck. This deck was actually the roof over a cabin area located in the stern section of a sailing ship's main deck.

Shipbuilders of the day, often designed this space, called a poop cabin in the very rear of the ship. It extended a few feet above the level of the main deck, and was finished off with a flat timber roof that formed a useful observation platform. The flat roof of the poop cabin also served as the place where the captain, officers and high-ranking sailors would find an ideal vantage point for observing the crew at work or to assess the ship's sails, since the poop deck was usually positioned behind the shorter third mast, or mizzenmast. The ship's captain, even if not at the helm himself could generally be found on the poop deck issuing orders to the helmsman.

So it was that passengers gathered in this area to worship. What church could be grander than that which had the sky for its roof, the ocean for its floor and God Himself as it's architect.

Great was the thankfulness of most, who after a week of sickness and dis-comfort, assembled to praise and worship Him who "*sitteth above the floods.*"

From that day forward, throughout the voyage, services including Holy Communion were administered.

The weather during the first part of the voyage was delightful.

Tom and Grayson spent time in conversation but the subject that Grayson had been most keen to engage in, had not yet eventuated despite his best efforts to contrive it. Grayson was most anxious to know why it was that Mr. Sutcliffe should feel so bound to render a return favor to his grandfather. After all that was the main reason it seemed to the young boy that he was on this sea voyage in such company. He did however often ponder the rather pleasing memory from the train trip when Tom had said that he *"liked him a lot."* This was a thought Grayson was glad to have and put some stock on, since it made him feel that he was not being merely tolerated by his older companion.

On Wednesday the 18th, the passengers had a beautiful view of Porto Santo, one of the Madeira group. This same morning Tom and Grayson joined the passengers in an anxious moment on deck as a fire alarm in the after-hold galvanized the crew into speedy action. This occurrence was seriously unnerving but it particularly seemed to unhinge Thomas in a rather curious way that Grayson was later to make a pointed observation about.

"So the fire was something that made you frightened wasn't it? Never thought you would be frightened of anything Thomas!"

"Fire is something that deserves a healthy respect son…I reckon it's unleashed as much pain and suffering as anything I know."

Fire at sea was a truly a great peril and a feeling of thankfulness had swept through the assembly as it was swiftly brought under control.

Two days later Tom was on deck pointing out to Grayson the famed peaks of Tenerife Palma and a little later, Ferro, the southernmost of the Canary Islands.

The skill of navigation was a constant source of wonder to Grayson as he contemplated how the captain and crew knew the right direction to steer the ship in.

After the 26th of September, having passed by the westernmost of the Cape Verde Islands, they saw no land for eleven weeks.

The sight of land after such a long time of just seeing ocean was very heartening. Due to the curvature of the earth, for sailors looking across the horizon, any land even in clear conditions, would be invisible to them for almost one hundred miles offshore. Seasoned sailors recognized land far off in the distance as it would be announced by a thin strip of cloud on the horizon.

To Grayson this was an unnerving experience to be sailing out into vast stretches of ocean and not see anything beyond the sea…one day after another…more sea. The motion of the ship was not as much of a problem at this stage of the journey as it had been initially. He had time on his hands and often sat in a daydream wondering what his mother was doing. He wondered if she missed him. He wondered how aware his father was of this voyage. Posing such questions to Sutcliffe didn't really help Grayson a great deal as he generally got lean answers bare of anything of substance, nonetheless, Tom was a fairly good listener and expressed empathy for the boy's circumstance and how he might be feeling.

Staring out across the sea in early October, Grayson was the first to see a tiny sail on the horizon.

"There! Look another ship!" he cried, alerting some of the crew in the appropriate direction.

The ship was a sister vessel to the one in which they sailed, making the same journey to the same destination. A brief opportunity for greetings alongside one another was afforded and then the captains pursued their chosen tacks to soon become dots on the horizon to each other again.

Grayson had thought often of death and pondered the life hereafter. Such thoughts were bought vividly to the forefront of his attention when about six weeks after having left England two small children died in the night. They had apparently been unwell even at the outset of the voyage. To Grayson it was a sobering experience to see the parents grieving as the little bodies were laid out for being *"committed to the deep"* after a brief service. It made a lasting impact on him and he spoke to Sutcliffe about it frequently.

"Do you think my Papa and my Mama would cry very much if I should be stitched up in one of those bags?" he asked poignantly.

Tom Sutcliffe was a wise man knowing how to give a prudent answer with honesty.

"I should think it would be a dreadfully sad thing for any parent to lose a child."

"But isn't it sort of the same really because they *have* lost me haven't they?" Grayson's active little mind was perceptive beyond his years.

"No they haven't really lost you Grayson…you're just in another place," countered Sutcliffe adroitly.

"But when a child dies they are in *another* place too aren't they?" persisted Grayson thinking about the talks he'd had with Tom about heaven.

"Well, er it's a different place but …it's not soo, so final…" was Tom's faltering response. "I mean you can still write letters and contact your Mum or your Dad should you want to."

Grayson stopped in his tracks, arrested by this new thought which curiously nobody had ever even mentioned to him up to the time he had been getting prepared to sail away.

"Do they want me to write a letter?" he asked, struck by the possibility that they might not and how he might feel should he not get a reply.

"You should certainly write a letter now and then as you choose."

That night as Grayson lay with the ocean swell gently rocking his hammock, the ship surged its way across the Equator in the dark. It was inconsequential to this young passenger who lay awake thinking what he might say should he ever write a letter to his parents. Why hadn't it been suggested he wondered? He didn't think he could ever write to Grandpa. What would he say? It occurred to him also, that the notebook with his father's writing in it lay still unread, tucked away in the suitcase. It could keep for another time.

He fell into a restless sleep as he lay wondering if they missed him back in London. Like the parents crying for their children who had gone to *"another"* place, did they cry very much for him or was his absence not especially noticed? He hoped they thought about him as much as he thought about them.

On October the 23rd Tom was standing on the deck with Grayson and explaining to him a basic overview of longitude and latitude. He pointed in the direction of west and told Grayson that Brazil was straight ahead that way and told him of the great city Rio de Janeiro. Tom Sutcliffe was a keen student of things nautical and geographical and Grayson appreciated the time he took to explain such matters. In Tom's sea chest, locked away were maps, charts and other papers that Tom occasionally hauled out. Each day there were lessons to be taught and when the ship crossed the 'meridian line' on November 1st, Grayson knew what Tom was on about.

Grayson was somewhat intrigued with the chest and its contents. Unlike his own meager little collection of belongings, Tom kept an interesting assortment of items in there. Once when Grayson had asked what the *"P"* stood for in the carved initials *"TPS"* on his chest, Tom had exhibited a strange, slightly evasive reaction and said he would talk about it another day. This was a very odd response. The explanation was not to come for quite some time and when it did, it would prove to be under the saddest of circumstances.

Rough weather made for unpleasant conditions for the next part of the trip as the ship rounded the Cape of Good Hope and headed in the direction of the new home the passengers were bound for. With the passing of the Cape a new milestone had been reached and the waters of the southern ocean beckoned the way to New Zealand. Although a formidable journey still lay ahead, anticipation began to surface that the next land to appear on the horizon would be that of their new homeland.

Excitement erupted on board the decks on Wednesday 11th of December when at about 5 o'clock in the morning, members of the crew first sighted the shores of New Zealand. Passengers straggled their way on deck to catch a glimpse of Stewart Island, New Zealand's smallest and southern most Island coming into view 94 days after having sailed from Plymouth, England. It was only at this juncture in the voyage that Grayson had the temerity to begin questioning Tom Sutcliffe about where they were going to live and what it was like. It was a matter of trust for Grayson to leave such details with his caregiver...and trust him he did. Grayson was curious but didn't push for information on such matters ...until about this point in the voyage. For some reason Tom had not offered much information at all in this direction, preferring to allow the little boy to find his timing and come to peace about such things when he seemed ready. It seemed that Grayson began to give clear evidence of just how ready he was for answers with the frequency and probing nature of the questions he would ply Thomas with day after day.

Passengers would never forget the jubilation on that beautiful day when they first beheld the magnificent mountain peaks of the Southern Island of New Zealand and the following day when the ship ran in close enough for some to almost long that they could land on the lovely sea beach backed by the low cliffs. That evening a glorious sunset settled over the snowy peaks of the Southern Alps and gave indescribable pleasure to one and all.

The scenic beauty sailing along the eastern and northern coast of Bank's Peninsula continually drew fresh gasps of wonder from passengers as they beheld the panoramic delights unfolding before them. Tom pointed out to Grayson on a map the landmarks that he was somewhat familiar with. When Godley Head came into sight it was not long before they would sail into Victoria Harbour with its rolling encircling hills that ran down to the water's edge.

On Tuesday December 17th, 1850, almost 100 days to the hour from the time she left Plymouth, England, The **Sir George Seymour** came to anchor in Victoria Harbour, Port Lyttelton, Canterbury, New Zealand.

It was Grayson's tenth birthday.

4

FROM SHIP TO SHORE

An air of excitement was prevalent as the passengers stood on the decks surveying the scene all around them. Beautiful shimmering, sparkling waters, sheltered by hills covered in magnificent greenery sloped down into the sea. Distant calls from native birds that he had never heard previously, echoed across the bay and around the port filling Grayson with awe.

Leaning out over the topside handrail on the starboard side, Tom pointed out to Grayson the recently built wharf and jetty which was the main disembarking point, with the new customs house standing nearby. It was over a year since Tom had been here and the dramatic changes that had rapidly taken place in that time were astonishing. This truly was an era of opportunity and fresh challenge.

Tom's enthusiasm for returning to this place with all its potential kindled a little spark of anticipation in Grayson. But it was only a little spark. Those feelings of apprehension still ran deep. Yet the newness and sense of discovery at least held at bay, the brooding melancholic silences Grayson would fall into at times. But who could blame him though when everything that had happened to him was taken into consideration?

"What a way to celebrate your tenth birthday!"

Tom beamed barely able to contain his delight, his moustache *"twitching"* as he gesticulated, throwing his arms around pointing out the landmarks. Pausing, as if suddenly remembering something, he put his hand into his pocket and drew out a little item. He gave Grayson a small black felt purse with a drawstring on it.

"Happy birthday Grayson."

Grayson took the purse expectantly. Holding it in the palm of his hand, he felt its weight and wondered what this surprise could possibly be. Maybe it was a watch similar to the one Tom kept in his waistcoat pocket on a chain…

"Thank you Tom," he murmured gratefully as he fiddled the draw-string undone with excited little fingers.

Gently shaking out the contents, a beautifully crafted little brass compass fell into Grayson's cupped hand. Hinged, it unfolded into a finely engraved and carefully produced instrument that represented the most accurate *"pocket technology of the day"* as Tom described it. Grayson had learned the value of a compass during the sea voyage when Tom had given him navigation lessons and taught him not only the value of a compass, but the need for one to calibrate their bearings from the stars above. They'd spent numerous nights staring up at the inky blue-black skies scattered with stars that sparkled on clear nights like jewels. Grayson had learned a lot about such things and was always willing to learn more from Tom. He'd learned about the wonderful order in the heavens and how sailors for generations had been able to navigate great distances by observing the stars. He'd been told that everyone needs a "compass" and what foolishness it would be to "sail" the oceans of life without anything to guide you.

Grayson had understood the lesson and grasped the significance of what Tom had been teaching and the point behind the gift that had just been given to him.

"It's just so great …really it's beautiful…thank you very much," Grayson said admiring the treasure he had been honored with. "I'll keep it forever…"

The long row-boats were starting to take passengers ashore and Tom stood in line with Grayson waiting for their turn to climb down the wobbly rope ladder. All the larger items of personal luggage, such as Tom's sea chest, were to be put on the foredeck and to be taken ashore separately once passengers had disembarked. Hand held luggage such as Grayson's small suitcase were fine to be taken on the row-boats. Grayson sat in the prow with his little case at his feet as the oarsmen began to pull away from the ship.

Not far away from the jetty areas, could be seen the wooden Immigration Barracks which had been constructed to house the new arrivals for a time. Small basic huts known as V-huts were also built quickly and simply to accommodate the emigrants until they found their feet. Some even lived for a while in tents around the Immigration Barracks.

Two other ships from England were in the port and another was due to arrive in a few days. All of them carried emigrants under a scheme devised by a group called the Canterbury Association that was one of a number of private company immigration schemes that would populate areas of New Zealand. With support from the elite of English society, as well as clergy of the Church of England, this pioneering settlement carried the ideal of transporting English society to a new land.

Within a year, a further fifteen ships would arrive bringing the population of this settlement to more than 3,000.

Tom Sutcliffe and Grayson thus were part of an organized European settlement program under the Canterbury Association that saw most settlers set up homes in or about Lyttelton or Christchurch.

In London, settlers applied for land in the new colony. For one hundred and fifty pounds, they had the choice of a rural block of 50 acres or a town section of one-quarter acre. They had the opportunity to participate in one of the "selection days"... a system whereby sections of land were issued by ballot in the new towns. The most popular sections at first were those in Lyttelton but then others moved over the Port Hills to be a part of the settlement in Christchurch.

Tom had thoughtfully considered his options and chosen to look beyond town and opted to buy a rural section. Relying on some work experience he had gained as a young man, he had plans to develop a farm in an area on the Canterbury Plains called Riccarton. This area had been established as farmland in 1843 by Scottish brothers, the Deans, who built the first European house on the Plains and named it after the parish they came from in Scotland and the nearby river, the Avon, after a stream on their grandfather's farm. Several other families were also working farms in this location supplying vegetables, dairy produce and mutton for Christchurch.

The ships stayed in port for several weeks while goods were unloaded. As passengers disembarked from the ships, they were greeted by dignitaries and notable office holders such as Sir George Grey, who happened to be the Governor General—the Queen of England's highest representative in this new colony.

The settlers were shown to the barracks where they were to be accommodated and offered hospitality as the newcomers to this temporary settlement. It was a large sturdily constructed timber building, not at all sophisticated, but it was comfortable shelter and a nice change from being at sea.

Being ashore felt strange though when at rest…almost as if the sway of being on the ocean was somehow indelibly imprinted on you deep inside. A pleasant change from being on board a ship for so long was the food. Fresh vegetables and meat along with dairy products were items one greatly appreciated when such items had not been available at sea.

That first night Grayson did not sleep much. Here he was, thousands of miles from what had been his home, on his tenth birthday in a new country, attempting to sleep on a wooden slatted bed in a temporary immigration facility accompanied by a man who was looking after him because his grandfather had arranged it.

Would his parents be thinking of him on his birthday? He missed them. Rather, he missed what he had wanted them to be in his life. He tried to imagine his father giving him a carefully chosen and wrapped gift, smiling approvingly.

Thoughts of his father made him think about reading the handwritten journal. Grayson still did not want to read the contents of the leather bound book that lay in his suitcase. He wanted to feel safe and reading whatever the words had to say might take that away. It was too much of a risk for now. There was no hurry and anyway it wouldn't change anything to read it some time later.

Lying in the dark, he briefly scrolled through a few random thoughts that he had been musing over…lines that he had practiced mentally as he wondered about putting a letter together. Should he take a chance on writing? Would he get a reply? His thinking drifted towards his mother as she had waved goodbye at the window over three months ago. He visualized the image he had of her strained face looking out as the coach had pulled away to take him to the railway station. He wondered why it might have been so hard for her to simply run down the steps and give him a big hug and a kiss.

As a child, Grayson's grasp of what his mother had gone through was naturally restricted by his lack of years and his limited perspectives. How could a nine-year-old know what a wife might have felt to have discovered that what she had believed about her marriage was a myth, inasmuch as her husband had deceived her and established another marriage and family behind her back?

For Grayson it was simple…he missed his mother badly and he was confused at her seeming agreement that he should be sent away because his father had been doing wrong things. Frequently his mother's photo was pulled out of the suitcase and gazed at wistfully. He longed to be loved…not just tolerated. He needed to feel he was special to his father and to have his approval. These were things he was deeply uncertain of and it provided a continual source of anxiety. Tom had explained wisely and appropriately to Grayson the breach that his father had committed against his mother, trying to re-assure the hurting boy that the issues were not about him…that he was loved in spite of clear history pointing to how it had been inadequately expressed.

With Tom's help, Grayson had gathered as best as one his age could, that his father had struggles of his own. Grayson's inclination to think he was the cause of every problem in his family relaxed a little once he had been informed about some issues that his father had struggled through with his parents during childhood. Thomas offered just a few fragments of detail now and then on the difficult background his father had and it served to alleviate to a small degree the sense that Grayson carried of *being* the source of all his parent's issues. He wanted to think the best of his father and appeared reluctant to hear anything at all that might put his father in a bad light. Nevertheless hearing just a hint of his predecessor's painful history alleviated Grayson's tendency to wear the blame for everything that was wrong in his family.

Tom had said he *"liked"* Grayson on the train as they travelled to Plymouth and how this drowsy little fellow, even in this moment, enjoyed the feeling that still came with recalling having heard those words. He loved to replay that conversation in his head ever so much.

Grayson looked over at Tom, snoring lightly with his coarse blanket half covering him and half draped on the ground. It wasn't cold and Grayson thought about how warm it actually was. Back in England, the month of December would have brought winter cold, but here, half a world away in a different hemisphere, it was the opposite season. Everything was strange.

Watching Tom sleep, Grayson reached under the pillow and held the little compass he'd been given as a birthday present. It felt good just to hold it. It was an unusually special and precious gift. Given the fact that it was his *only* gift made it even more significant. He considered the lessons he'd received while at sea about the importance of a compass and the analogy Tom had drawn of how foolish people are to live out the journey of life without one.

Grayson had understood the analogy. He felt a drawing towards wanting to have the friendship with God that Tom talked about.

Grayson was grateful for Thomas Sutcliffe but was scared when he thought about how vulnerable he would be without him. It made him consider how life might be right now if something should happen to Tom. Grayson observed that the strength of faith Tom had, seemed unshakeable and it appeared he was confidently anchored in a relationship with God that was personal and translated into everyday realities. Tom prayed a lot. Not just lines out of a book but spontaneous conversational talking, was his style. Grayson was impressed with that—even if at times it might seem he was just speaking words into the air. This man appeared to possess connection with "Someone" who he trusted to never let him down. Grayson fretted for that kind of stability since he had discovered even in his few years, that people who should know better, can let you down... and he wanted to be loved in such a way that every fear of *ever* being let down again would disappear.

Grayson felt a sense of safety with Tom. He was strong, yes in body, but also in his convictions about right and wrong. He called things the way they were and could not tolerate pretentiousness. It was not in a judging way that he expressed his opinions, but he was firm and clear about them in a way that it made sense to insist that people do the right thing. Such convictions flowed out from the values he lived by, as a person wanting to be a friend of God. Tom talked about it frequently in very personal terms...it was not just in a religious way, but in a way you would expect a person to talk about a friend who they loved and whose character they could describe with affectionate detail.

Tom stirred, rolling over in his bed and clunking his hand on the heavy wooden sea chest alongside. Grayson had become aware the chest was crammed full with various things such as clothing, papers and books along with a few assorted tools. There were those mysterious carved initials *"TPS"* which he had still chosen to avoid engaging in any direct conversation about.

Grayson's attention fixed on the letters visible in the dim light. He was still curious about them as well as the strange reaction Tom had displayed when he'd been asked for an explanation. Come to think of it, a number of things lingered in Grayson's mind that he would like to get some straight answers from Tom about. He still was anxious to know what the real connection was between Tom and his grandfather. How had his grandfather had such influence with Tom to compel him to take Grayson away? He had chosen not to raise these matters again for now, resting in the assurance that Tom had said, one day he'd talk to him about it.

Thomas...Sutcliffe. A reasonable assumption perhaps...but was it *"Patrick", "Paul", "Phillip"* or a host of other names Grayson could think of? What name did the *"P"* stand for and why the unnecessary hesitation in offering a simple answer?

5

MAKING A NEW HOME

Tom had spent time in the New Zealand bush previously and from that experience, had described what the *"dawn chorus"* is, to Grayson. It was the early morning wake up call of a myriad native birds so prolific in the mid nineteenth century as they coo'd, sang and whistled their welcome to a new day as it broke. Tom had explained how New Zealand was the very first place on the whole planet to see a new day dawn and the sun rise over the earth.

The *"dawn chorus"* was an example of creation exulting in the Creator, Tom reckoned. While they weren't presently in heavy bush or densely forested area, there was still enough forestation around the port in spite of the clearing that had taken place, for the birds to give Grayson a wonderful welcome as the sun began to rise on his first day in New Zealand. It was so unlike anything that could ever have been heard in a London suburb.

He lay there in this faraway place listening to bird life calling an invitation to participate in a new day that was dawning. It would be nice to feel as chirpy as those birds, Grayson thought.

After downing a filling bowl of lumpy porridge that was served from a communal canteen, Grayson was allowed to accompany Tom who had been invited to be included in a party being taken by some important gentlemen over the difficult Port Hills road from Lyttleton to Christchurch in a couple of horse-drawn carts.

Their purpose was to show Tom and another person the parcels of land that they had been allocated and they planned to be back in the barracks in a couple of days. On returning, the heavy luggage would be sent at that point by small boat around to the Estuary and up the Avon River that flowed into and through the town of Christchurch. Even though the travel was uncomfortable and arduous at this time, the mood in the party was cheerful.

This was the culmination of several years worth of planning that had its beginnings in early 1847 with the Canterbury Association being formed to establish a settlement and townships before the settlers arrived. Part of the plan included the opportunity for the new settlers to buy land and this would supply the money for public works such as roads and schools.

Governor Grey had sent the land commissioner Henry Kemp to the South Island in 1848 to buy land from the indigenous native Maori people. Many chiefs had signed "Kemp's Deed" agreeing to sell certain lands, keeping some for settlement and reserves and for those places where they gathered food. A surveyor, Captain Joseph Thomas was sent to choose a site for the Canterbury settlement and he had planned three towns—Christchurch, Sumner and Lyttleton.

Christchurch would later become New Zealand's first city in 1856 under the terms of a royal charter. This was because it was the *"seat"* or base for a bishop who was installed by the Archbishop of Canterbury. The successful building of the Christchurch Cathedral would follow, built in the central square of the town as a hub with all roads radiating out from the square in a grid-like fashion.

The site of Christchurch has three dominant landscape elements by way of its natural geological formation; the flatness and expansiveness of the Plains, moderated by the volcanic Port Hills to the South and then looking to the west the distant relief of the outlying foothills and the ranges of the Southern Alps that are snow covered in winter.

For Tom, being in this place was the beginning of the fulfillment of his dream. Over the next day or so, he would have the chance to look at the place that would be his new home and to select some of the farm animals he hoped to purchase. Constructing a house and other buildings, breaking in land and running a few sheep and cattle to start with along with selective cropping would keep him busy.

Having his own farm and living off the land, Tom would have the opportunity to extend the holding by leasing further lands. Cattle and sheep runs were looking very promising out on the Canterbury plains with wool sales particularly starting to grow significantly in the 1850's.

The plan was that Grayson would do some schooling with some other settler children under the tutelage of a local schoolmaster and work on the farm with Thomas.

Bumping and swaying, the party lurched their way to the Christchurch settlement over the rough Port Hills "road"...a rather grand name for this track hewn out of the forested hillside and strewn with stone and rocks. It was still a work in progress and a test for both the horses drawing the carts and those hardy souls occupying them. Tom could easily understand why many travellers going to the Christchurch settlement opted to go by boat along the coast and up the Estuary that narrowed into the Avon River. Wending its way through the district, this waterway was a pleasant and vital thoroughfare providing access and making newly opened up areas serviceable.

Horse drawn carts and wagons still frequently labored their way over the hills route but larger items were inevitably transported around the coast and up the Avon River by boat. The rigors of the Port Hills road compensated the traveller with beautiful scenic bush and spectacular views along the way. Even though the original forest and native bush was sadly no longer pristine having been somewhat cleared and in areas replaced with tussock, at this point in time, the distinctive sights, smell and sounds of native New Zealand bush still provided a delightful distraction on the uncomfortable journey.

It would not be that many years later when it would be a different story as a more drastic approach to clearing forest cover was taken in the name of progress, sadly with the resultant loss of native bird species and other creatures such as native bats.

Descending the slopes of the hills and viewing the northern plains spanning out before him with the distant relief of the Southern Alps in the west, Thomas Sutcliffe was suddenly struck with the enormity of what he was doing. It seemed bigger, vaster and more daunting than he remembered from his previous experience of this country. Usually very upbeat, he found himself nervously wondering what he had let himself in for as caregiver to a ten-year-old boy, entering into a sale agreement on a parcel of land that he had not sighted, along with the uncertainty of the actual scope of the task he faced in developing his land.

Dismissing these fleeting flutters of apprehension he reminded himself of the careful decision processes he had followed as best he could, to arrive at this point now. Also, there was a high level of trust involved in purchases such as his and after all, the terms and support offered were very favorable as the Canterbury Association made every effort to assist the settlers due to the keen interest they had in seeing the colony succeed.

Once over the Hills and onto the Plain, it was past three o'clock in the afternoon when Thomas and his party approached the settlement of Stratford. This particular settlement had replaced a settlement that had been originally proposed at the head of Lyttleton Harbour. Due to the realization that there was insufficient flat land to meet the Canterbury Association's requirements around that former site, the area of Stratford that the party was now arriving at, had become part of a much preferable location. It was a natural choice. Stratford was at a point where those coming up the Avon first encountered land that was slightly more elevated and it was therefore drier ground by comparison with the swampland that stretched extensively beyond as far as one could see.

There it was. The fifty acres of land that stretched out before them and this was what comprised the Thomas Sutcliffe "estate".

It was all his and he had the deeds to prove it.

Thomas leaped out of the cart. Stretching his back for relief, he stood there with a mixture of nervous excitement and great pride. Here was the piece of land he was prepared to pour his heart and soul into developing as an income-producing farm.

He would put his mark on it.

A few others had done the same thing starting with the Deans brothers who had established their farm not far away at Riccarton some seven or eight years previously. Thomas was equal to the task and he could do it too. He would need to work hard clearing part of his land of vegetation including areas of swamp forest. It would then have to be drained, cultivated and fenced.

A natural building site for a house and implement sheds was not far from the track where the carts had come to rest. The others in the party slowly clambered down. A surveyor among the group stood by Tom unfurling rolled up plans and pointing out to Tom with a piece of stick that he had picked up, the perimeters of this proud new owner's land.

A wide grin seemed to have permanently fixed itself to Tom's face and as Grayson trudged wearily to join him, he jubilantly grabbed the boy by the shoulders, pulling him closer while patting him and exclaiming repetitively…

"This is it. Right here. This is it right here in front of us. We're here!"

Tired from the bumpy exhausting day of travel Grayson mumbled appreciatively the best way he could, in agreement. He could see Tom's obvious enjoyment at this moment and tried hard to join in. That same niggling feeling he had felt periodically of not really fitting in, of being an intruder, of being an accessory forced upon Thomas, seemed to surface. After all what did he really have to rejoice in?

Graciously the brave youngster attempted to hold back his feelings.

"It's very nice and I'm glad to see you so very happy. I can see your animals on it now and I can see your crops growing too."

"Yes and we'll probably build the home in a way that we get some shelter in that area right over there," said Tom pointing to a stand of beautiful, mature trees.

"The winds can blow with powerful force here I'm told," he continued, "there's the hot dry *nor'wester* in the summer and strong cold southerlies which can even bring a hint of snow is what they've said."

"The trees are very nice," Grayson mumbled trying to be polite but unconvincing in concealing his total lack of passion.

Picking a slight reticence in the boys voice and manner Thomas' smile faded as he pulled Grayson to him suddenly feeling slightly sick inside. He suspected correctly that the little boy was struggling with a sense of *"where do I fit in this?"* In a flash Thomas accurately discerned the huge sense of displacement such a young life might feel at this point of time even though he personally was so excited standing there at the threshold of his dream.

After all, this little boy most likely was too scared to even have his *own* dreams now since so much had been taken away in recent months. How might it feel to be wrenched out of your natural family and taken away from everything that was familiar, being forced to accept a new home, a new environment so very different in another part of the world…wondering if you were special to anyone anywhere or even missed? Of course he would be fearful…how could he not be? Grayson's struggles with feelings of worthlessness and lack of self-belief even extended into uncertainty about simple matters such as wondering if it would be all right to even send a letter back to England. These were all major occurrences and issues which Grayson had to face as an outflow of the decisions that had been made for him and which he had no choice or say in whatsoever. These were major dealings for any person much less a child just turned ten years old.

Feeling somewhat self-conscious at having become aware of the puzzled eyes of the other members of the travelling party on him,

Thomas quickly re-gathered his thoughts and emotions from having become temporarily distracted.

"I'm glad you're here with me and we will make it all work out… you and me together," said Thomas quietly pulling Grayson close to his side again.

"My home will be your home…you'll see. I'll look after you just like I've been telling you."

Thomas looked down at the sad little figure huddling against him and his heart went out to him. Dropping to a squat to be at eye level, he ducked below Grayson's cap and saw tears trickling down the boy's cheeks. Grayson buried his face in his hands since he was flustered to have been "caught" in an emotional moment. It was all too much for him and he sobbed quietly as Thomas wrapped his strong arms around the little chap pulling him in close.

"Come on there…it's alright…" he said gently drawing Grayson's clasped hands away and running his finger up the boy's cheeks to catch the little rivulets.

Thomas reflected on his strangely hollow words knowing deep down inside that it really wasn't all right no matter how re-assuring he tried to be. How on earth could it be all right? What he was witnessing was grief and it was entirely valid. The sense of gut wrenching, deep loss that Grayson felt was something Thomas Sutcliffe understood and in measure had experienced personally. He had been there. One day he very much wanted to tell Grayson about it so that the boy would understand that his pain and struggle really was understood. However offering some kind of insight as to his own story would have been inappropriate at that moment, he reasoned inwardly. He couldn't do it now. For the present they were in company.

Thomas would keep his story for yet another day.

6

A WAYWARD SCHOOLMASTER

By late February 1851 considerable progress had been made on the Sutcliffe property. Thomas had attacked the project with great enthusiasm and boundless energy. It had been a very warm summer even by Canterbury standards and for an English immigrant it had proved to be a bit of a shock to the system. But where there is desire, there is motivation and Tom had busied himself fencing, digging endlessly and tirelessly to drain and cultivate the land.

A straightforward wooden farm cottage typical of this colonial period was on the agenda and an order of timber was arranged that could be picked up from the mill anytime soon. Once materials were in hand a start on construction would be possible.

Grayson wondered just how much money Thomas had in that chest of his. In reality it was a modest sum but by carefully managing his funds, he had prudently purchased a dozen sheep, nine cows and a couple of beef cattle. From such humble beginnings he would establish his farm. He had found a beautiful chestnut mare that was available for purchase and a small serviceable carriage for transporting goods and equipment.

So very much had happened since Thomas and Grayson had sailed into Port Lyttleton just before Christmas. They had stayed at the immigration barracks for a little over five weeks during which time, they had made the trip over the Port Hills and back on several occasions as well as accessing the property by sailing into the Estuary and then coming up the Avon River. The rugged Port Hills road was something any traveller tried to avoid if they could. It would not be for a good many years to come, that a rail tunnel *through* the hills would be completed in 1867 to link Christchurch with Lyttleton.

Now Thomas and Grayson were living on the land in a large tent. Being summer it had not been a problem but Tom was aware the cooler autumn was not far ahead and it would not be many months before winter followed. So the house construction was a priority. It would be small to begin with and could be extended and added to as time and budget allowed. Tom had drawn a plan for the simple double gable "A-framed" style dwelling with a low deck covered by a verandah-porch over the front entrance.

Neighbors were not abounding at this point, yet they were steadily growing in number and those who were around and about were generally abounding in goodwill and helpful neighborliness. Thomas and Grayson had on quite a few occasions had the chance to offer spontaneous hospitality to callers who came by to make themselves known to the new arrivals in the tent.

Following one such visit, a neighbor returned over several days bringing in loads of smooth locally sourced grey river stones which were placed in a pile awaiting the building of a fireplace and chimney. Others would bring some item such as cheese or a lump of freshly baked bread.

Some friendly local native Maori people coming by the property happened to have been carrying a large quantity of eels apparently caught in nearby waterways. The eels were strung together in bunches with strips of a strong rope made from the flax plant and didn't look like something the average Englishman would naturally relish. In their easy-going way, these Maori folk stopped by and did their best to converse with the new arrivals. Before leaving they gave Thomas and Grayson a few eels to cook in the embers of their campfire. These people were skilled in traditional cooking methods and wrapped the eels in broad flax leaves and showed them how to cook this delicacy. This was food that would prove to be much better to eat than it was to look at!

A merchant by the name of George Gould sold supplies and provisions as the proprietor of the first little settlement store in the community and it was from here that Thomas bought bags of seed potatoes and other types of seed to sow in the soil that he had been carefully cultivating on his land. There was a steady arrival of ships supplying a flow of immigrants and the demand for vegetables, fresh meat and dairy product encouraged Thomas Sutcliffe that he had a viable market for the things he hoped his farm would supply.

Grayson was helpful and generally worked to perform a range of chores assigned to him. He was a fast learner in all things and Thomas was keen to see him commence some formal schooling now they were settling down.

The first school had opened in Lyttleton on January 6th 1851 under the leadership of Reverend Henry Jacobs. Thomas had taken Grayson along but he had not been enrolled there since their final move over the hills was imminent to begin developing the new farm. Besides, there was talk of a new school being established in the near future quite close to where they would be in Riccarton. Grayson would be enrolled there.

Towards the end of April the farm cottage was taking rapidly shape. Its timber structure was plain but certainly there was a rustic "pioneering" appeal about it. The eastern gable end had an impressive external chimney made with the river stones cemented together running up to extend just beyond the roof ridge. Inside it was very simple, with a fireplace being the central feature. There were three rooms off the one main room one of which would be the parlor or food preparation area. The two other rooms were bedrooms—one for Grayson that was small, but it was neat and inviting.

The typical outdoor privy had been the first vital piece of construction on the land and would continue to provide its imperative function long after the cottage was completed. During the building of the cottage, it proved habitable enough to move into while the work was being completed. It was stark and far from finished with scant furnishings apart from beds, however it was a big improvement on the tent. Getting inside had become increasingly imperative with the arrival of cooler temperatures and the ageing tent, with it's fabric falling to bits was tatty, draughty and beyond further repair.

"There's something important that I want to ask you that I have been thinking about," announced Grayson one morning, his brow furrowed in concentration. He had been somewhat pensive for a day or two.

Caught off guard and always somewhat anxious about the lines of questioning Grayson was capable of, Thomas stopped in his tracks, his heart strangely pounding hard in his chest.

"Alright then," he said drawing his breath. "Well what is it that's been on your mind?"

"You might not like it," Grayson warned considerately…a warning that did nothing to alleviate the anxiety and slightly defensive stance building in Thomas. What could be stirring in the boy's head now?

"Try me," he said bravely.

"Well…um there's something I want."

Thomas found his mind racing about what might be coming. This was a boy who to his credit, was a compliant child never asking for anything much. Could it be some wild thought he was incubating about wanting to return to England? That was a door that was firmly shut. Was he going to press for a conversation in areas Thomas was not prepared to offer yet? What would be forthcoming?

"*Chickens!*" blurted out Grayson. "I've been thinking I would like you to let me keep some chickens and you could have *all* the eggs!"

With a visible sigh of relief Thomas relaxed, feeling an instant sense of weight fall away. *Chickens.* Was that all? Why had he got so worked up? Of course the boy could have a few chickens.

"Of course! Anything…chickens would be grand…and so would some eggs be!"

Later Thomas would reflect on how the episode had highlighted the fact that there were some underlying tensions in this relationship with Grayson. Not tensions of conflict but there were places where some open and honest communication just did not exist. He knew it could create a greater sense of ease to have things in the open. There were areas they needed to talk about. There were things Grayson needed to know. It was awkward at times, such as when meeting new people, almost always the assumption would naturally be made that Thomas, was Grayson's father. And it was always the same…then if he's not the father what were the circumstances that led to them being together in the antipodes? Onlookers with questions could not be blamed for it certainly did seem a bit of an odd duo.

With Grayson about to start at the little school that had commenced, no doubt the questions and speculation along these lines would need to be faced in a real way.

Arriving at the quaint little wooden schoolhouse on the appointed day he was to start school, Grayson predictably felt a little shy and tentative. Of course most children do on their first day at school, so Thomas assured Grayson.

It went well…at least it seemed to, as Grayson began to settle into this new routine. The schoolmaster, a Mr. Pickett, was a tall, thin, hawkish individual with balding head and gaunt, expressionless face dominated by enormous bushy, greying eyebrows that were like verandahs over the pince-nez spectacles that were often as not, clasped on the bridge of his nose. He carried a satchel each day and wore an overcoat irrespective of the weather, which he shed upon arrival at the schoolhouse, hanging it on a coat hook in the corner behind his desk. A tweed suit was all Grayson ever remembered seeing Mr. Pickett wearing and his presence was always announced by the distinctive smell of tobacco all about him, for Mr. Pickett smoked a pipe—never in the classroom, but everywhere else it seemed to hang from his tight thin lips. The pipe sat on the schoolmaster's desk during class and his pupils grew accustomed to the odor it gave off—even when not in use. Whether or not the pipe had some bearing on the matter or not, Mr. Pickett was a bachelor. He kept to himself in the community and while he commanded some respect because of his station, this ageing schoolmaster caste a lonely shadow while maintaining a hint of mystery about his personal life and indeed his past.

He appeared to be a gracious and compassionate man in spite of those slightly intimidating eyebrows and he demonstrated some empathy for the ten-year-old, most recent addition to the ranks of his class. It was clear he seemed to find it difficult to grasp the nature of the relationship between Thomas Sutcliffe and Grayson James Pollock.

Mr. Pickett was curious about his new charge and his interest in Grayson as a student was clear from the outset. This scholarly schoolmaster had an impressive record of achievement from England's finest halls of academia. That he should be found teaching in a colonial, semi-rural schoolhouse with a string of University degrees was somehow an incongruent match.

His curiosity grew as he began to press for more insight into the relationship between Thomas and Grayson. Nobody noticed this interest was developing in any way that was unwarranted. Grayson was a very bright child with a gift for learning quickly and an exceptional capacity for retaining new information. Curiously, here was a teacher whose qualifications and knowledge would have been a rare find in this pioneering settlement. But there was a history to this schoolmaster that had anyone been aware of, it would have precluded him in any way at all from contact with *any* young male pupil.

First it was the offer for extra tutoring…Grayson was glad of the teacher's offer for coaching him on a personal basis and to be honest, slightly flattered that the schoolmaster should pick him above others to have the extra tuition.

Thomas Sutcliffe was generally a very astute and careful guardian, but only in hindsight saw that Pickett's interest in Grayson went beyond a sincere desire to help advance a young boy's education. Thomas had done a superb job under the circumstances in walking with Grayson through the inner turmoil of being caste off from family and all that was familiar. In no way could he be held responsible for what was to happen. Thomas would always carry a lingering doubt that he should have done more, that he could have communicated a little more freely and perhaps circumvented the happenings which eventuated.

Grayson was a vulnerable target and he had no appreciation of the reality that he was being carefully groomed by a predator. He somehow exuded to the schoolmaster's perverse eye, the fact that he was a child with deep pain and hurt inside, with emotional longings that for the most part were unmet. With probing questions under the guise of a caring heart and listening ear, Grayson began to fall prey to Pickett's own confused and lost emotional world.

The older man began to skillfully contrive opportunities where predatory advances would begin to take place in solitude. Shocked and bewildered, Grayson who had always been a compliant child, now found himself being manipulatively silenced under threat that all future lessons would definitely cease should he talk to anyone or think of disclosing their *special* friendship. And so an already floundering child began to sustain further wounding, having become subjected to Pickett's inappropriate physical advances.

Grayson withdrew into the horror of a dread-filled, numbed state. Thomas observed the change and sought carefully to understand what might be going on. Silenced under threat of all schooling ending, Grayson deferred to the schoolmaster's placations and justification for being secretive. At times it almost seemed reasonable and plausible. Such is the nature of deception and lies. But no amount of smooth talk could dispel the screaming shame Grayson felt and the boy's inner protests could not be silenced.

Suspicious questions had been posed as to why such an academic man should have to leave his country of origin and they were about to be answered. Evidence was beginning to surface that would seem to confirm the rising suspicions had some validity to them.

Grayson had become a significant concern to Thomas. The boy began resisting any attendance at school. He was scarcely eating and had become decidedly withdrawn. The classmates had noticed that Grayson was being singled out for the increasingly overt attentions and favors of Pickett and some of the children had begun speaking to their parents about what they were observing.

There were fourteen students enrolled in the school at different ages and levels of learning. While lessons were taught corporately in an open classroom, the skill of the teacher would ordinarily enable pupils to progress at a rate commensurate both with their age and natural ability. The basics for a rounded education were supposed to be taught equally to all pupils during the five-hour school day. But a decidedly unhealthy connection on the part of this schoolmaster had been formed with Grayson…and now it was showing…

Grayson was bright academically and had started out attending classes as anything but the reluctant schoolboy. But now he refused to go near the schoolhouse in spite of every strategy Thomas deployed. Pleading and forcing didn't work and even taking Grayson there personally in the morning was futile. As soon as Thomas left, the child too would leave and wander about aimlessly for the entire day, afraid to be at school and anxious about going home because he knew Thomas would be unhappy.

All of this was too much for a man with a strong protective instinct like Thomas and after about a week or so, he made up his mind as to what had to be done.

It was a day that had dawned clean and crisp. He walked on the crunching frosty ground with a determined stride. Today he would confront Mr. Pickett with a demand for the truth as to what had happened to Grayson…for an acknowledgement of what Thomas somehow sensed was really going on. Pickett always arrived early and Thomas on this occasion would be ready and waiting.

The smell of pipe tobacco announced the arrival of the schoolmaster long before he came into view. Slightly stooped, head down, the lanky over-coated teacher walked towards the door of the school. Thomas paused cautiously until he heard the key in the lock before stepping around the corner and addressing Pickett.

"A few words with you Mr. Pickett!" Thomas said directly causing the startled teacher to gasp in fright.

"I need to know right now what it is that has been happening between yourself and my Grayson...the boy's attitude to classes has completely changed and I believe you will know the reason."

"How ddare you...why hhowhow ddare you lie in wwait for me and atta attack me in this way!" Pickett retorted, stuttering and stammering self-righteously as he tried to gain some self-composure.

"Any chance you had sought for a cccivilized conversation would have bbbeen granted but now I will give you no such audience."

Thomas realized the man was completely unhinged by his approach and pressed his point.

"You have no choice in the matter because I am having an audience with you right now! Tell me what you have done to Grayson...I demand your explanation as I believe Grayson is a victim in precisely the same manner as those ones you have probably interfered with in England and as a result had to leave the teaching profession!"

It was a bold strike based on nothing but guesswork-however it was a strategy carefully contemplated and it found the mark. The schoolmaster's face turned ashen and his jaw dropped open. Stammering and stuttering he began to feebly protest.

"Howw, how dddare you, How dare you bring these fantasies... this is outrageous...yyyooou have no idddea what you are saying...I will, I will have you pay for this outrage...!" Pickett's voice began to rise in crescendo until it was a shrill hysterical shriek.

The response was exactly what Thomas had expected and it told him everything he wanted to know. Now he would move to the next phase of his plan that would be to involve other parents of children under the tutorship of Pickett who would corroborate in forming the picture that was emerging.

Later that afternoon there was a knock on the door at Thomas' little home. It was the first of the parents Sutcliffe had sought insight from on the matter of the schoolteacher.

"Mr. Sutcliffe, I'm happy to talk to you about your young fellow Grayson..."

It was a Mr. Barker accompanied by two other fathers. Thomas knew the Barker family and liked this man. His daughter Emily had been kind to Grayson and shown care for him when he was first settling into the class as a newly arrived pupil. She was a sweet, kind-hearted little girl with an eye for noticing the "underdog" or anyone marginalized.

"What is it that you need to say about Grayson?" Thomas asked feeling a sense of urgency rising within him.

"Well my Emily has been telling me about the strange way the schoolmaster is behaving around the boy. Mr. Pickett is a clever teacher no doubt but there's some of us now who have heard enough and we also want to ask some direct questions," Mr. Barker continued.

"And who might 'some of us' be then...?" asked Thomas.

"Other parents. This is not gossip sir...this is hard for me to do but there's something odd happening here...there is something occurring that is just not right between this teacher and your boy!"

For the next half hour Mr. Barker and the other visitors recounted the observations many of the pupils had talked to their parents about and it cumulatively painted a picture that things indeed were not right. Even if the remote possibility existed that it was nothing to be unduly concerned about, it surely could not hurt to at least clear up the issue in a civil manner. The men shook hands agreeing to call for a personal meeting to ask Mr. Pickett for explanations.

"I'm obliged to you Mr. Barker...I appreciate the manner in which you have stood with me in this matter which has come to my attention because God knows the boy's behavior has been completely beyond my understanding of late."

Thomas spent a restless night tossing and turning without sleep as he thought over the circumstances that had prescribed the necessity of the following day's meeting with the schoolmaster. He chided himself unnecessarily for not having been vigilant enough to anticipate a situation that apparently had developed. What might this added injury do in the life of young Grayson?

"God you know I've tried with this boy…You alone are the all-seeing One…please, will You intervene and let justice prevail…heal any damage done in Grayson…" he prayed silently as the dark hours scrolled by.

The very next morning a delegation of four parents including Thomas Sutcliffe and Mr. Barker went to meet Mr. Pickett. They arrived well before class started for the day and waited patiently until an audience with Mr. Pickett was possible. The teacher appeared busy preparing the class lessons for the day and was not at all warm to the idea of receiving those waiting to speak with him. His aloof and somewhat defensive approach from the outset introduced a confrontational element to the dialogue. The presence of Thomas Sutcliffe in the deputation would have been cause alone for Pickett to embargo any meeting.

"Away with you lot and your kangaroo court!" Pickett spat cynically toward the waiting group.

"There is most certainly not a speculative attack on you here sir," said Mr. Barker to the testy schoolmaster.

As the nominated spokesman he continued, "We would merely like the chance to gain a better understanding about some concerns that have been presented about the ways it appears you relate in particular with your pupil Grayson."

"Grayson is a fine pupil and I want him to succeed as he has ability that easily matches any pupil I have ever seen in my career," snapped Pickett raspily.

"That may well be so," Mr. Barker continued, "but there are now way too many concerns that have become apparent about the scope of the attentions this boy is receiving from you sir."

They left with Thomas having insisted on an agreement being reached that the same delegation would address the concerns with Mr. Pickett the following day, meeting at half past 3 o'clock in the afternoon. The schoolmaster firmly asserted there was no need for any meeting since he had no case to answer to but would use the meeting to prove this to the parent's satisfaction.

The meeting was never to eventuate.

An empty, locked schoolhouse greeted the pupils the next morning and there was no trace of Mr. Pickett. His belongings had been emptied from the desk he occupied and it became obvious that it wasn't just that he was running late for class…he'd gone.

Completely disappeared.

Initially there was no evidence of Pickett or his belongings at his lodgings but later a crate of books was to be discovered in a storage shed on the property where he had resided as a lodger in self contained accommodation.

Investigations later indicated that a man, reportedly matching Pickett's description, had made his way to Lyttleton and at first opportunity, this person had boarded a ship bound for Australia. He was never traced but it was believed to be likely that he had disembarked somewhere there, although nobody knew that with any degree of certainty. Which part of that vast country the fugitive schoolmaster ended up in, would remain an unsolved mystery…

For Thomas there was further work now in trying to ensure that Grayson felt safe and was not judged guilty for having any part in the abuse that he had innocently fallen prey to at the hands of his teacher. The formerly eager pupil did not want to return to school and that did not matter because it would be a little over two months before a new schoolteacher could be engaged and then another month before she was to start in the role. Grayson began to talk openly little by little and a clear picture of the abuse he had experienced emerged. Gently Thomas sought to "rebuild" Grayson and to externalize the pain that he had been caused. It was slow but he did seem to progress, although the withdrawn wariness that exemplified Grayson, seemed to have been further entrenched.

A deeply resentful rage simmered against Pickett in the community of family's served by the school and it had been vowed that any replacement would be have to be very carefully and thoroughly investigated.

Fortunately those who had been appraised of the situation felt nothing but sympathy for young Grayson and of course nobody ever considered there could have been any complicity on his part in the matter. It mattered a lot to Thomas as well, that people did what they could in terms of showing their support and acceptance. He welcomed their expressions of inclusiveness and encouragement directed towards Grayson.

By the time Miss Willoughby, the replacement teacher came Grayson was making very good progress and was ready to tentatively venture back to school at the same time the new teacher was starting.

She was well spoken of and received into the community with warmth due largely to the fact that she was an open, outgoing person unlike her mysterious, reclusive predecessor.

Miss Willoughby was a firm but kind-hearted woman in her late forties. She had spent some time studying in France and in Italy, acquiring a great love and knowledge of literature and art. Once again, here was a teacher who took a shine to the winsome, intelligent little boy whom she had received a comprehensive brief about. But this teacher, while recognizing there were indeed abilities in Grayson that were well above those of the average student, was careful to find in *every* child that which was to be encouraged and fostered.

All her children knew Miss Willoughby was there for them without any mixed, self-serving motives.

7

SALVAGING THE STUDENT

Grayson's new schoolteacher did a lot to rebuild his confidence.

She was a big-hearted woman and her larger than life personality was matched by her larger than life physical presence. In spite of her loud way and her matronly domineering size, she was a very tender, sensitive person possessed of a gentle, almost maternal manner. It was this that reached Grayson and touched him.

Maternal care was something that for obvious reasons presented as a considerable deficit in his life. Grayson had always ached to feel what it might be like to know his mother's love. He thought of her often and wondered if she ever thought of him. The memory of her sitting in the window seat as he left home, was forever etched in his mind. It was a picture he had no answers for, since it gave him no indication of what her emotions were towards him. A lurking sense of betrayal around the fact that she had not stood up for him or fought on his behalf left Grayson very confused. *Was she sad he had been sent away? Did she miss him as he much as he missed her?*

These were questions that were actually to haunt him all his life.

Miss Willoughby was not his mother but she did begin to, in a certain way, fill the areas of void that Grayson's absent mother had left. She was capable of being motherly and nurturing, at the same time he was under no illusions that she was a soft touch. She was anything but that. This matriarch of the classroom did not tolerate any approach to schoolwork that was less than each student was capable of.

Miss Willoughby was an excellent blend of both authoritarian and disciplinarian while simultaneously exhibiting teaching skills that inspired each one of her pupils to do their very best. Grayson began to recover his love of school.

And then there was Emily Barker, the eleven-year-old daughter of the courageous father who had initially fronted up with Thomas about the Pickett situation and helped Thomas bring things to the light. Mr. and Mrs. Barker had sailed with their family from England on The **Charlotte Jane.** One of the first of the four ships leaving Plymouth with Canterbury Association emigrants, it had coincidentally sailed within hours of The **Sir George Seymour**, the ship which Grayson and Thomas had sailed on. When they arrived, The **Charlotte Jane** was already in Port having arrived a day or so earlier.

Grayson had never spotted Emily amongst the sizeable crowds of newly arrived emigrants at Port Lyttleton and their paths had not crossed at any time during the transitional stay at the Immigration Barracks.

Of course Grayson knew Emily since she had been at school as he had begun in the class under the old schoolmaster. She had been kind and consistently thoughtful in her relating to Grayson but he had not particularly noticed her.

Something however changed apparently for Grayson and from about the time Miss Willoughby took over the role as schoolmistress, it was clear that he had indeed noticed her.

Having done so, he was thus more than happy for any chance at all for their paths to cross should the occasion ever present itself.

Emily was a cute little button with golden curls that fell around her face in a tousled sort of a way. Too thoroughly shy to be overt in his awareness of Emily, Grayson was polite in every way and discretely kept a respectful distance while always remaining eager to find ways for her to notice him.

Sitting in class, the school desks were arranged in such a way that Grayson could see Emily...but not so as she would be aware of his frequent staring. There would be odd times when sensing she was under scrutiny from some quarter, she would turn to catch his eye on her and she would smile at his red-faced attempt to nonchalantly avert his gaze in another direction. Grayson's little crush on Emily probably had more to do with the fact that here was a girl who by dint of personality was outgoing enough to take the upper hand and to initiate innocent, friendly conversation. It was all very innocent and really rather normal but it made Grayson feel special since he would have invariably shrunk to the shadows finding direct conversation hard to engage in.

Without her being the outgoing gregarious child that she was, Grayson may in all likelihood, spoken hardly a word to Emily and just become one who *admired* her from afar. Nonetheless, Emily did see the good qualities in Grayson and she came to like his quiet thoughtful ways. Although too young to see it as a worrying feature, the introversion and certain mystery about him, made Grayson interesting. The situation that had been forced upon Grayson by the former schoolmaster was explained to her in such a way, that even without a full disclosure of the details it caused Emily to look at this young boy favorably for appearing to be able to come through tough circumstances and survive. It appealed to her that he was not a rough, boisterous and rude boy like others. Besides he was very clever too and Emily liked that about him.

"You want to come and see my chickens one day Emily?" Grayson ventured hopefully with a coy expression on his face one morning as they arrived at school.

Pupils converged on the schoolhouse by 10 o'clock coming from a wide catchment by horseback, horse drawn cart and numbers walking quite long distances.

"They're only a few days old the ones that just hatched and they are very fluffy," he continued awkwardly.

"You can even hold them," he persisted observing little obvious response.

"Thank you for asking me, I shall see." Emily replied politely giving little away. She was not particularly encouraging but neither was she dismissive.

That's the way it remained for the rest of that year. She wasn't ever to come to see his new chickens but Grayson remained friendly and was not unduly perturbed and showed no ill feeling or sensitivity at his invitation not being received enthusiastically.

Emily was to leave the school at the end of that year. Grayson expected that he would miss her greatly no longer being one of the pupils in attendance. Her family planned to leave the area to open up a big sheep station further inland. Back country runs were being offered for sale at very good prices and the sale of these runs gave the newly formed Provincial Council a regular source of income. Canterbury was prospering in these years with wool exports steadily increasing the amount of money available in the province.

In the following couple of years, numbers making up the pupil role from the wider community would increase and the school structure changed somewhat to grade and stream the students. Another teacher was engaged to help, but Grayson continued to find special affinity with Miss Willoughby who had been so understanding of his shy withdrawn manner when she had first begun her tenure with the school.

Once Emily was no longer in attendance at the school, Grayson discovered that he missed her more than he had thought he might and it surprised him. Her absence left something of a void that ought to have been predictable enough given that in reality, Grayson was quite a distant, solitary figure and he struggled socially. Although he was most certainly not an unlikeable child, he did not readily draw others to himself in companionship or form friendships readily.

"Will I ever see Emily again?" Grayson had asked Thomas reflectively when Emily had left.

"Why, there's every decent chance you could well do," he replied without much certainty.

"You always lose the things you want most…" Grayson glibly stated leaving Thomas pondering the conclusions that the experiences of life had already forced on his young charge.

Grayson's disappointment over Emily leaving the school produced in him a sense of loss and isolation. She had been his only real friend in the classroom and while she was everyone else's friend as well as his, Grayson felt he was just that more important to her than the others. At least that was what he had hoped. She had made a special point of saying goodbye to Grayson claiming that she was not going away because she wanted to, and that had pleased him.

Grayson knew about decisions being made for you by adults and had told her just a little bit of his story. It had felt scary to start with and yet it was good to have someone who he felt it was safe to be with, giving him the chance to be heard. And now she was gone. Finding his voice was not something Grayson was accomplished in, but he had found talking to Emily was made easier by her attentiveness and bright personality. She had made attending school for five hours a day just that little bit more interesting.

But now she had moved and life had to go on too.

Miss Willoughby continued to see in Grayson a boy with ability and potential. While not very skilled socially, he was a pleasant fellow, prone to being introverted but with a depth beyond his age. The teacher had quickly noticed that Grayson was a boy whose academic prowess showed in obvious ways. He had a remarkable gift for detail and retention, clearly evidenced when she found he had committed to memory many of the poems in a school journal containing about two-dozen of the English romantics works.

"Grayson you have the ability to go a long way in your studies," she told him one day. "Would your *father* agree to letting you carry your study further and having the opportunity to advance further with some additional school-work?"

Miss Willoughby found Grayson a considerable challenge both in terms of relating to at a personal level but also in terms of generally interacting with him and stretching his ability. As his teacher, she found his capacity and appetite to learn was exceptional. While Grayson's quiet, reclusive personality held some appeal, it was a two-sided coin for it also required constant effort extracting any level of meaningful communication in order to gain a better understanding of this boy.

Seeing Thomas Sutcliffe arrive at school on occasions with Grayson, Miss Willoughby naturally enough assumed him to be the boy's father—an assumption made by a good many people on any first meeting.

Because she knew of the discrepancy with their surnames from the school roll, it was of interest rather than necessity that Miss Willoughby sought to find an explanation. She wisely bided her time over the matter until she had an opportune moment to press Thomas for a little background understanding.

The Pickett episode had been described to her in detail but the detail about Grayson's family life and the nature of his arrival in New Zealand had remained somewhat cloudy to her.

"Thomas is *not* my real father ma'am," Grayson said bluntly in response to Miss Willoughby's question.

"I believe you should have the chance to get the very best education you can Grayson. Would he be the one to have to agree to you pursuing your studies and even perhaps going to University one day?"

Curiously, like her predecessor, Miss Willoughby was also one who happened to wear little spectacles on the end of her nose. Staring over the top of them at Grayson, he blushed self-consciously and squirmed uneasily in his seat. She had no intention at coming across as overbearing but her zeal to see Grayson move forward in achieving what she sensed was his potential, provoked her to risk this forwardness.

"Thomas talks to me about the future but he does not force me to do things," he said choosing his words warily.

In essence Grayson had of course been forced to come to New Zealand in the first place. He wanted to stay in England. Others had different plans for his life but that was not the doing of Thomas.

"Many farm owners plan for their sons to carry on from them and I didn't know if Mr. Sutcliffe may have such plans for you Grayson. I would like to talk with him about this."

She had a point. The colonial life initially was not heavily weighted in the pursuit of academic matters. There was rather, an emphasis on manual work, on developing a new community with hard work and effort. In a decade, that situation would change and no longer would higher education be something that just happened in England. The Collegiate Grammar School (later to be known as Christ's College) had opened in Lyttleton back in April the year before. Perhaps Miss Willoughby had this in mind as the next logical step in advancing Grayson's education.

It was now mid June 1852. Grayson was not even thirteen years old yet and too young to be influenced by news of the Australian gold rushes. It did however prove to be very attractive to young men from the Canterbury settlement to travel across the Tasman Sea to seek their fortunes. Some were very young, possibly destined for higher education but the majority of these young men were the work force either for public works such as roads and other development as well as casual labor for farms. Their flight slowed the development of public works somewhat over the next three years, creating a shortfall in the availability of labor.

For Thomas Sutcliffe there would be no such distraction as gold fever. During the coming years he was to continue to consolidate his farm and extend his holdings to develop a very thriving little business.

It was 1855 when Grayson decided to end his schooling to the very great disappointment of Miss Willoughby. She suspected direct coercion from Sutcliffe had influenced her protégé but there was no substance to this. Thomas had exerted no influence whatever on Grayson in making a choice about his education. Perhaps Thomas could have offered a little more enthusiasm in the conversation about the possibility of university and an academic career, but he wanted the boy to reach his own conclusions. Grayson certainly had the ability for such a direction but chose happily to work for Thomas. He was young enough to pick up studies again should he choose to do so. For now he threw his weight in on the Sutcliffe property.

New settlers continued to be a ready market for the farm produce and it was a time of prosperity.

In the same year Grayson stopped attending classes, "assisted immigrations", or the payment of the fare of selected workers or emigrants under the Canterbury Association scheme, was taken over by the Provincial Council. Appointing an agent in England to promote the cause and select the emigrants ensured a steady flow of thousands of new settlers.

The prospects for the future looked positive and Thomas Sutcliffe was satisfied that the dreams he had for coming to New Zealand were on target. His unshakeable trust in the providence of a God who ordained the details of his life anchored him in a confident optimism.

As for Grayson…he had already experienced enough in his young life to know that there are sometimes unexpected twists in the journey.

And he was to experience a few more yet.

8

A TRAGIC ACCIDENT

The shroud of silence had persisted. Thomas had not really opened the lines of communication and for his own reasons, adeptly side stepped the possibility of being cornered by Grayson's probing questions. He felt bad about this. Any day soon he planned to give Grayson a letter he had carefully written to spell out some things he would struggle to explain in a conversation. It was an honest attempt to open dialogue. Thomas Sutcliffe was an honorable man and could not stand accused of many faults among his peers…nonetheless his procrastination and reluctance to deal with Grayson in a completely open fashion, while understandable, was not helpful.

Now as a seventeen-year-old, Grayson thought less about his parents but there were times when it ran deep. Feelings of bitterness and cynicism would arise and somehow that shadow over his life prevailed. It was like a blanket of shame that seemed to make him feel some inner sense of inferiority…internally Grayson was aching…it was like he was almost always on the defensive inside…like he owed the world an apology for existing.

The little bound journal from his father was still lying in the original suitcase under his bed. Curiously, it still remained unread, and so it would remain—relegated to a place where it could not be bothersome. It was not a case of him not being interested…but he was wary. It could hurt him and why would you open yourself to that? Grayson had picked up the diary many times, turning it over and over in his hands. An internal battle waged as he contemplated delving into whatever it was that his father might have wanted to say. But it was too terrifying. What if it disclosed things about his father that he did not wish to know…?

Grayson wanted desperately to believe the best of his Dad and preferred to live in a state of shutting out anything that might jeopardize the unreal, idealized image he had, or that might paint his father in a negative light.

Little did Grayson know that within the journal's hand-written pages, there lay a message that potentially could change his entire life around. Yet sadly, he always decided it could wait for another day. It so tore at his soul, that one day Grayson nearly threw the book into the fireplace. So shocked was he at his reaction, that he secured some twine and carefully wound it around the journal then tied it off, as if to provide a deterrent to ever picking it up spuriously to have a read of its contents.

The picture of his mother was on his bedroom wall, vacantly staring into space in a way that revealed nothing of any emotion good or otherwise. It was just a face Grayson would try to convince himself at times. But this wasn't just *any* face and inside he writhed with unresolved anguish and longings periodically. Of course she loved me he would tell himself. But how could he reconcile the facts of what had happened with being brought to New Zealand with a mother's love? Being here was very hard to comprehend…So many questions were just stuffed down inside… with no answers.

He had neither written nor had anyone written to him. Grayson had decided he wanted the initiative to come from "home" with any letter writing and so he waited, practicing the composition of letters he would like to send sometimes in his mind. The question of whether they cared about him back in England or not, had in his mind, been answered by the passage of time. Thomas Sutcliffe had received one letter in six years from Grayson's grandfather while he had written several times himself.

Thomas Sutcliffe and Grayson Pollock were an intriguing and rather odd little twosome among the growing settlement. Always well liked, Thomas had earned a place of respect for being a hardworking, honest man of integrity. Grayson had no friendships of any depth, just acquaintances, appearing "self-contained" and insular. Apart from Thomas, Grayson had no one who he had any particular sense of relationship with.

And now even that was about to change.

It was early one morning. While it was routinely planned in advance, the trip into town delivering vegetables and farm produce was usually uneventful. There was little that one would ever anticipate that could go wrong.

Thomas would drive the horse and cart into town with Grayson assisting to unload at the various points along the route.

What was about to happen was completely unexpected and it came with a suddenness that gave no one any chance to intervene.

Lugging a sack of potatoes off the cart deck onto his shoulder, Grayson heard the commotion before he saw it. Somewhere in close proximity, there was shouting and desperate cries accompanied by the noise of hooves pounding down the carriageway. He knew it was close and getting closer but Grayson's attention was diverted seemingly on getting the bulky load onto his shoulder and into the merchant's store across the road. The potatoes on his shoulder blocked his vision significantly as he stepped out, turning slightly to try and see what was going on.

A wild-eyed horse, nostrils flaring, had been startled somehow and now in sheer, blind, unstoppable panic was rushing at break neck speed pulling an unoccupied cart precariously through the settlement! About to step out into it's path, before he could even react, Grayson heard Thomas yell and simultaneously he felt himself hurtling through the air to land with a thud on the ground, potatoes spewing all around him. Dazed and bewildered, Grayson sat up on the dirt to see the bolting horse with cart flying behind it, disappear around the bend.

And then he saw Thomas. He was lying motionless not far away on the ground. The realization registered with Grayson instantly as to what had just happened. He had been about to step into the direct line of the runaway horse and cart. Thomas, anticipating a horrific accident had dived at Grayson, hurling his whole body through the air to push Grayson clear of the charging horse. Clearly he had not escaped the pounding hooves and wheels of the cart himself.

"Thomas, no... Thomas..." wailed Grayson as in shock he rushed to his friends side.

For Grayson, everything went quiet in that instance. The deathly stillness that comes with shock hung in the atmosphere. It was only to last momentarily though as a vocal and desperate crowd, having either witnessed the accident or heard the noise, rushed to converge on the accident scene.

"Go get the doctor!" someone was screaming above the hubbub of yelling voices.

"Oooh Thomas...oooh no-ooo, Thomas no ..." was all that would come out of the lips of the sobbing teenager as he tenderly rolled the broken body of his friend over.

His eyes were closed but he was alive and breathing, though even to a layman, it was apparent that he had sustained serious injuries in his heroic effort to save Grayson from the fate that had in fact befallen him.

Lying there now struggling for life, the deathly pallor and thin trickle of blood coming from the corner of his mouth were indicators of physical problems nobody present quite knew how to handle. An air of deep sobriety took the place of the panic of a few minutes before.

Thomas moaned softly and his eyelids flickered as several men tried to ease his battered, bruised form onto a makeshift litter covered by a blanket.

Utterly distraught, Grayson followed as Thomas was taken onto the front porch of a nearby building to await the arrival of a doctor who someone had ridden at speed to fetch. Lying there he began to rally and appeared to regain a greater consciousness of his whereabouts and what was taking place, although he still showed signs of rapid, shallow breathing. A bluish color tinge was evident around his mouth. He stretched a hand weakly towards Grayson who was kneeling close by his side…lying there, it was very obvious in his eyes there was no fear…just a tender concern for the sobbing, hovering boy. Thomas coughed on occasion emitting a small quantity of blood that would sputter from his lips. He was clearly laboring and a noisy rattle attended his breathing.

At the doctors insistence Thomas was taken to a nearby lodging room after an initial examination. The doctor had arrived almost two hours after the accident with the bolting horse had occurred. He surmised Thomas had initially been concussed and had carefully supervised the stripping off items of the patient's clothing to enable a full understanding of the injuries to be determined. Trying to work out a treatment plan was futile without looking over Thomas and as best he could, he'd appraised the scope of his injuries. Bruising and cuts, one a bad gash to the forehead were relatively easy enough to treat… the concern lay with what he observed as evidence of serious internal injuries. A sickening indentation on the left side of his abdomen hinted at issues beyond the scope of a general practitioner's ability to bring a remedy. Reading Tom's rapid heart rate and breathing difficulties, he believed he had at least multiple fractured ribs and most likely a punctured lung along with smashed bones in his shoulder and a broken collarbone.

The doctor did everything he could to make Tom comfortable and then having left clear instructions for care and some medication for pain relief, he said he was going to seek the attentions of a Mr. Earle, Surgeon Superintendent of The **Randolph,** one of the larger ships that had bought settlers to the colony years before. No hospital existed in Christchurch until 1862 and while as yet there was no medical association, a fraternity among the few medical practitioners had begun.

Mr. Earle arrived early the next morning. Thomas had not deteriorated and had even made the effort to try to talk with Grayson who had stayed alongside all night. The boy had not eaten or had anything to drink and the physician made an appeal for him to take care of himself. Grayson wished it was he who was lying where Thomas was. Brave, noble Thomas Sutcliffe had been true to his word and put his own life in jeopardy to fulfill the promise he had made to Grayson's grandfather that he would *"protect the boy with his life"*.

The surgeon verified the doctor's conclusions but in keeping with the limited options of the day to deal with such injuries, decided against any intrusive attempt to assist the situation. Indeed, on occasions the best efforts of surgeons of the day might well have exacerbated matters in such an emergency and a conservative approach was deemed to be in Thomas's best interests.

Grayson's distress was compounded by a deep sense of self-recrimination and blame. Every accusing thought imaginable assaulted his tortured mind. He told himself that it was fully his fault that Thomas was in this state. *I should have never come to town...Should have been more careful...I am always the cause of every problem and trouble...I wish I had never born...I hate myself so much...*

Plagued by such tormenting thoughts, he had stayed alongside Thomas virtually since the accident…intermittently weeping, pleading and whispering his apologies and pledges of affection. It was a heart-rending scene to see this young man's guilt-ridden anguish as he crouched by his friend.

Thomas drifted in and out of periods of varying degrees of awareness. Several times he had looked steadily at Grayson and spoken clearly, unmistakably.

"I'd do it over again… told you back at Paddington I liked you… still do…and always…" he gasped breathlessly with a faint smile on his face as he recalled their conversation as they had left on the train for Plymouth.

"Don't die Tom…pleeeaase stay with me Tom…pleeease…be strong again," Grayson wailed in uncontrollable agony feeling the full weight of anguish that helpless despair can bring.

"This is…I'm ready for…not sure you are…I've got …and you must…you…" his labored breathing made it difficult for Thomas to gasp his dying message to Grayson. The boy felt sure that Thomas would be talking about the issue of facing life beyond death as he had heard Thomas often talk about his personal assurance of having eternal life. Men save for the last the things which mean the most to them and Grayson had learned emphatically from Thomas about where he stood on such things…about a personal choice to be made…a choice he'd urged upon Grayson at various times to put faith and trust in Christ as His Savior. It seemed probable that Thomas lay poised on the brink of slipping from this life into eternity and yet he appeared peaceful. Grayson was witnessing the confidence of a man assured he was heading for heaven.

The faith Thomas spoke of had been demonstrated by a lifestyle consistently lived out. But for now, this young man grappled with answers as to why this had been allowed to happen…His eyes misted with tears of grief and his heart pulsated with a mix of anger and frustration.

Later that day Thomas deteriorated. He made less effort to communicate and lay there pale and motionless. The occasional coughing had caused him to still splutter blood… some was dried into his moustache. Grayson looked at Thomas remembering a very different day when that same moustache had seemed to "dance", his face wreathed in smiles—the day they had first seen the farm. How happy Thomas had been then with that big grin and giant moustache spread all over his face.

Thomas was not distraught. In fact, in spite of clear indications of enduring pain and discomfort he seemed to be genuinely at peace. He seemed to know what was ahead because he began fumbling for the key on a cord around his neck that Grayson knew opened the lock on the large sea chest at home. It caused him a few moments of awkwardness, fumbling in the direction of the key. Tilting his head to the side ever so slightly, Thomas looked earnestly at Grayson with an amazing look of love and tenderness in his eyes that Grayson would never forget. There was no hint of anguish or distress on his face.

He closed his eyes and breathlessly wheezed out, "Take it Grayson…it's all in there…it's there for you…please. I love you… Thank you Lord…. Grayson remember *everything*…please…"

With that, there was a sound of air escaping from his lungs and his spirit left his body.

Thomas slipped peacefully into eternity—ushered into the presence of his Lord whom he had loved and served.

9

MAKING SOME ADJUSTMENTS

Two days after Thomas' funeral, Grayson sat at home on his best friend's bed. How he ached. Looking around the room, the place just "smelled" of Thomas. His vision, his hard work, nothing would even be here without Thomas. And now what was left for Grayson? In his current state of dejection the future seemed bleak and unappealing. Those feelings of being lost and the sense of abandonment and shame now combined with the heavy guilt that somehow he might have been responsible for the death of Thomas. He wished he could talk with someone but there was really no one who would understand.

His thoughts drifted to his parents and his grandfather. Unless he wrote to them, they would be unlikely to ever be aware of what had taken place. He had still not completed a letter although on several occasions had attempted to write one. Neither had he received one. Walking from room to room, Grayson's attention became fixed toward the photo of his mother on the wall as she stared benignly into nothingness. Looking at the photo, Grayson mentally discarded the idea of writing.

How he missed Thomas. It was like a physical ache. Thomas Sutcliffe was a remarkable man and had been a fathering, mentoring figure all wrapped up in one. Thoughts about his parents since the death of Thomas, served to further the sense of void and rootlessness

Grayson felt inside. Losing Thomas was completely life shattering as he had little idea in the midst of his lonely grief, as to where to go and what to do next.

Maybe he should go back to England? Would they welcome him there? What would his father do with an estranged son? Were his parents even alive? What had become of Grandpa?

Questions poured through his besieged mind continually. And there was so much he would have liked the chance to say to Thomas and things he still wanted to ask so badly. It seemed there were just so many loose ends.

Taking the key out of his pocket that had been around Thomas' neck, Grayson looked over at the chest, locked, sitting in the corner. In one hand he held the beautiful little compass Thomas had given him on his tenth birthday…the day they had arrived in Port Lyttleton almost eight years previously. In the other hand, he turned the key over and over, tears spilling from his eyes. Dropping to his knees he crawled to the chest, wiping his eyes to see sufficiently to slide the key into the lock. It felt almost like a strange violation. Here was the chest that held so much mystery for Grayson and for which he had somehow held a sense of respect for, since it was private and the property of Thomas.

Creaking the heavy lid open, an envelope on top of everything else caught his attention over and above any other item that was in there. On it was written, in the writing of Thomas himself—

For Grayson James Pollock
PRIVATE & CONFIDENTIAL

This was a large beige envelope, unsealed and it begged to be opened. Grayson's fingers trembled lightly as he slid the pages of a letter out from the envelope. His eyes flicked nervously over the hand-written pages and his heart thumped loudly as he folded the letter open on the floor and prepared himself to begin reading. A lump came to his throat and he swallowed hard when he noticed how recently Thomas had prepared the letter for Grayson. It had been dated less than two months previously and it was obvious the intention Thomas had in mind was for it to have been given to him personally at some point.

My Dear Grayson,

I have wanted to talk a good deal many things through with you and feel I may have failed you in this. Forgive me for now broaching the subject in this manner but perhaps it will open some things for us to talk about. This seemed to me a way I could begin this conversation with you and it may of itself answer some of your questions.

There have been occasions when you have questioned me about your grandfather, how it was that I was appointed to be your caregiver when the decision was made that you should accompany me to New Zealand. This decision was one that was made by your grandfather in accordance with your mother's wishes. I do not believe your father was informed of the plans and I remain uncertain to this day, if he knows of your whereabouts.

Much of what you have experienced, I believe I understand since in some ways it is not too dissimilar from my own story.

As an eight year old, I lost my family and your grandfather took me and gave me a home since there was no family member to care for me. My parents and your grandparents had been very best friends. They had holidayed to the coast and we were staying at an old inn. One night a fire caught the building and my parents perished in the blaze. You will remember when we were sailing to New Zealand, how much the fire on the Sir George Seymour caused me alarm and I was concerned for your safety. Perhaps memories of my childhood experience accounts for that.

On the night of the fire at the inn, your grandfather risked his life to rescue me from the upstairs room where I was trapped. I suspect he never did forgive himself for not being able to rescue my parents as well as me.

Until I had grown and then began to travel, I lived with your grandparents.

Your grandfather was kind to me. You see now why perhaps I have felt I owed him a debt. I was raised with another boy who your grandparents had 'adopted' even before I came. His father had gone away abandoning him and his mother when he was quite young. Later on this boy's mother, (she was a relative of your grandmother) became unwell and died. As your grandmother was nearest of kin, she persuaded your grandfather to foster him...something he had apparently been hesitant about.

The other boy was eleven years old when I was bought to the home.

Grayson that other boy was your father. When I was bought into the home of your grandparents, I was about to turn nine-years-old, he was already there and had been since his mother had died. I was bought into the home and grew up under the same roof as your father and while it looked like we might be brothers, as you can see this was not the case.

He grew up using his family name 'Pollock.' I believe your grandfather struggled somewhat to accept him from the outset and many years later when he married his very own daughter (your mother), your grandfather found it hard to accept particularly since he felt their ages were very disparate. His concerns seemed to be justified when your father was later discovered to be in another marriage with children, while at the same time being married to your mother. It was at this point that your grandfather never wanted to see him again. He believed sending you with me was for your good, as well as ensuring he and your mother would not have any reason to ever see your father again.

I was ten when your mother was born to your grandparents and she was quite young when I left the home to study. She and I had not been very close although she regarded me as a 'brother' and I was happy to regard her as a sister although we were not natural family.

Your father had left the home earlier than me but in later years started returning on occasions and it was then his relationship with your mother began to develop. She was eighteen and your father was twenty-nine when they married.

A couple of other things remain for us to talk about. You have often wondered about the initials on my sea chest. Well the "P" stands for "Pollock"—obviously your family name, being your father's natural surname. Your question will be as to how I got the name too. When I was received into the home to be fostered by your Grandparents, your Grandmother insisted that the two boys she was raising should share some commonality and added 'Pollock' to be my middle name. She did this hoping we might find some brotherly bond, knowing it did not please your grandfather who saw it as a meaningless gesture since we shared no common bloodline. As a ten year old I had little care about the name being added and consequently it just stuck!

I will be looking forward to talking with you once you have read this and become aware of these things. I do hope that the conversation I intend to have with you soon might be helped along somehow by this letter.

There is only one more matter and it is this. I have no living natural family. You are my closest 'family'. I am almost an 'uncle' but I feel in many ways you have become like a son to me and so, should anything ever happen to me Grayson, everything I own and all my material possessions will become yours.

The greatest possession that I have is something I cannot give you. That is my relationship with God through the Lord Jesus Christ and the gift of salvation. This is a matter I have spoken to you about many times. It is my prayer and desire that you will not hesitate to claim this treasure for yourself.

With love and my deepest affection.

Yours truly,
Thomas Pollock-Sutcliffe

Grayson closed his eyes, stunned at what he had been reading. Knowing that Thomas had taken the time to write him a letter with a view to talking over issues and clarifying things touched him deeply. The fact that the conversation would now never happen filled Grayson with that familiar sense of abandonment.

While it was overwhelming for Grayson to receive such a letter loaded with information and revelations about matters that had been perplexing him for years, Thomas had been right inasmuch that the contents certainly did answer many of his questions. Grayson was touched as he observed how freshly written the letter was and reflected how awful it would have been to have lost Thomas without him having ever penned the words. He was grateful for the fact that Thomas had committed to written form such a record before the accident had occurred.

Over and over he read the letter. It was as if a jigsaw puzzle was being pieced together. Grayson cried on and off over a period of days, barely leaving the cottage and not having much desire for contact with the occasional visitor who would drop in, to see how he was faring, often leaving a small gift of some sort.

Grayson missed Thomas intensely.

In the weeks following he lay awake at nights wondering about what he should do. He thought about selling the property that had been left to him and returning to England. It seemed a pointless plan as there would be little for him to return to. But on the other hand Grayson felt there was little for him staying on the land too. He didn't have the passion for being a farmer and trying to maintain the property and manage animals on his own, was not working. Already it was evident the property Thomas had worked so hard for was going downhill. It was completely beyond Grayson and it added to his sense of failure and shame that he could not do Thomas proud with the upkeep of his property.

A solution came just before the Christmas of 1858. Grayson had had a very subdued eighteenth birthday spent in quiet reflection. Solitude was not very helpful to Grayson but it was what he wanted.

He spent time remembering vividly his first birthday in New Zealand, standing on the ship as they had arrived in port. The little compass gift, disembarking onto the rowboats, Thomas and his enthusiasm, it all seemed far-away and distant now as he pondered the future.

A knock on the door stirred him out of a convoluted maze of thoughts he had been lost in. It was Mr. Hopkins, the owner of the property adjacent to the land Thomas had left to Grayson.

"How would you be Grayson?" Hopkins asked extending a rough labor worn hand. "You been much on my mind since the sad loss of Thomas. 'E were a very good man."

"Well I guess I'm managing to get by I suppose," Grayson mumbled dispassionately, head down.

"I want to ask you something Grayson. I know the work in making a farm like the one you have stay in good shape…and I wondered, well I've been wanting to put a proposal to you."

Grayson scratched his head wondering what was coming from this usually cheery neighbor who was well known for his honest and enterprising way. Hopkins seemed highly nervous and hesitant as he continued.

"I was wondering if we might be able to sort something out that might be…well you know, a help to the both of us…if I'm intruding I am sorry but would you consider letting me buy this 'ere property. I would like to discuss an arrangement perhaps."

"What sort of arrangement are you thinking of…?"

"Well I am wondering if I bought the place with a deposit and paid you out the balance at, say a set amount each month… while at the same time you remained living in the house as long as you'd be a wanting…"

The farmer had his hat in his hands wringing it mercilessly in a self-conscious fashion, pausing only to wipe his mouth with the back of his hand occasionally.

"If you'd like to have tea with my good wife and me tonight we could talk some more to get some understanding and come to an arrangement perhaps Grayson."

Early in the next year it became legal and finalized. A price had been agreed upon for the stock and Grayson had sold the property as a going concern to the Hopkins family. He received a reasonable deposit, had somewhere to live without any expense to mention and a small regular income from the payments of the balance owing on the property.

Grayson stayed on for two years as an occasional farm worker, but his passionate pursuit lay in reading and study. It wasn't surprising when he told Hopkins he had a hankering for a change. In fact the desire for moving on gripped Grayson day and night.

10

COURTSHIP AND MARRIAGE

"Soo...Grayson, would you still be wanting to show me your chickens then?"

A lilting voice drifted laughingly over the top of the peripheral noise and spun Grayson around searching for the source. At first vaguely familiar, it was instantly clear when his eyes alighted upon a young blonde woman approaching him.

"EMILY!!!" shouted Grayson in unbelief. "Emily Barker!" he repeated excitedly.

She stood there, hands on her hips coyly smiling at him. Her eyes sparkled and her blonde hair hung around her face in a way that really hadn't changed much since they had been at school together. She had developed into quite a beautiful young woman and Grayson was not hiding at all well, how struck he was with her presence.

"My goodness, well I just can't…look at you. I mean…you really grew up…"

He felt foolish and clumsy in front of this confident young woman who seemed completely at ease, obviously enjoying his stammering professions of delight at seeing her.

"Well look at you too Grayson Pollock…" Emily said with her eyes roving over Grayson. He had grown to be a pleasant looking young man, not a husky build, but broad shouldered enough and someone whose presence was not entirely lost in a crowd.

The way Emily looked at him, made him want to draw himself to his full height and somehow make a better impression than he felt he might have made to that point.

"Guess we're not school children anymore then eh," he said cringing inside at how he could hear himself making such an inane statement. What a daft thing to say!

"The chickens got tired of waiting Emily," he said attempting to be witty with a dash of sophistication in his tone. Oh dear…it felt like he was dying inside as each time he opened his mouth nothing sensible seemed to come out.

What was wrong with him?

"Come over here and talk with me."

Emily came to his rescue and gave him a friendly pat on the shoulder and grabbed his jacket sleeve leading him over to a lounge sofa.

For nearly a year Grayson had been living in the central city.

Leaving and moving into the central city after staying on living for two years in the house that Thomas had built, was a good thing.

The death of Thomas had left a yawning chasm in Grayson. A desire for books and learning had gone somewhere to filling the sense of emptiness Grayson felt. It was precisely this that had led him into central Christchurch. He had initially worked in a bookshop and publishing house that gave him ready access to copious volumes and the chance to indulge his voracious appetite for books, to browse and purchase them as he saw fit.

Grayson's mind would drift back at times to his school teacher Miss Willoughby who had played a part in provoking his love for literature. She had believed in him and had seen clear evidence that he had unique scholastic ability. Her disappointment was obvious when he had elected not to pursue higher academic study and in part he was making up now for that decision. There were times when Grayson was disappointed with himself for neglecting to follow

Miss Willoughby's counsel and for not choosing to heed her well-intentioned advice and encouragement.

She remained an important influence in his life even though there had never been any further contact. Her warmth and motherly manner combined with her assertiveness, delivered something Grayson felt secure with. He liked her forcefulness whereas to others it was likely to have been taken as overbearing and pushy. To Grayson it felt safe. The fact was, this teacher communicated much more than met the eye to her young student about how a female figure, motherly, yet strong and in control could help him in the many areas in which he felt inadequate.

Grayson was not under any real constraint to find employment as he would still receive the payments against the balance on the sale of the farm for a little while. He had enrolled for a teacher's training course and was completing the required papers.

This was a time when the settler community enjoyed a reasonably buoyant economy and one of the signs of this prosperity, was the increase in the number of public buildings in the city—a significant one being the Canterbury Museum.

It was here at the opening function of the Museum that Grayson and Emily had now met again, seemingly by chance. Grayson had begun work under the Director, a highly respected geologist by the name of Julius von Haast. A clever man, this Director had used a significant find of bones in a swamp area called Glenmark, to the Museum's advantage. The bones were from 'Moa'-very large flightless native birds vaguely like a huge ostrich, which were believed to have been extinct for a long time. There was a number of species of these remarkable creatures—one variety evidently could have grown to stand several feet taller than a grown man.

By swapping moa skeletons for collections and specimens from other museums throughout the world, a creditable range of exhibits had been gathered.

"It really is terrific to see you again after all this time," Grayson said finally finding some measure of composure as he sat chatting to Emily. She had learned previously that Grayson worked at the museum, in particular with the *moa* project and had made a point of being invited to the opening. So it was not exactly a "chance" meeting.

Emily was clearly pleased to see Grayson.

Her little quip about *"seeing the chickens"* had of course been a reference to Grayson's cute attempt in their childhood to find an excuse to spend time with Emily...but now of course more latterly with Grayson being involved at the museum with huge bird bones, she had used her clever, razor sharp wit in reference to his work. It made a big impression on him.

Grayson learned that she had left her parents farm to live in the city and had developed a reputation as a renowned water-colorist, her work being highly acclaimed and well sought after. Emily was working on a number of commissions including an illustrative series of water-colors for a botanical book that a publishing house was producing to catalogue native New Zealand plants. She had a small "studio" where she lodged in the city and as it turned out, it was about a fifteen-minute walk to the Museum and not that much further to where Grayson lived.

There was a mutual delight in their making one another's acquaintance again. And there was much they wanted to catch up about concerning each other's lives since school days.

Over the next few weeks they talked often and spent hours in each other's company. Emily genuinely seemed to understand how Grayson had felt as she learned of the death of Thomas and the circumstances of him coming to New Zealand in the first place. This young man, nearly twenty-three years old, had some deep issues and Emily appeared to be able to draw some of those deep complexities from his emotions.

Perhaps he was a challenge to her. Grayson, although very stilted, certainly had a depth to him but there were bewildering times when he would just shut down inexplicably and withdraw. Undaunted, Emily would just share about her own life, her background and future dreams. She felt she was falling in love with this complicated young man who appeared to share similar feelings for her as well.

If it were ever true that opposites are attracted to one another, then anyone making such a claim would have had ample evidence to support the theory in this couple. He was very likeable, deeply contemplative and thoughtful, inclined to broodiness and somewhat socially reclusive while she was bright, talkative and irrepressible in her enthusiasm for living a sociable life to the full.

After quite a number of months, Emily had written to her parents about Grayson expressing her desire for them to meet him. Grayson nervously understood her desire to make the introduction and was enough of a gentleman to want to do the right thing by Emily and respectfully honor her father with such a meeting. Even though Grayson was experiencing confusion inside about his intentions at this relatively early stage in their relationship, Emily's confidence and enthusiasm seemed to carry him along.

In spite of his feelings of trepidation, Grayson believed he might be growing to love Emily and he was very attracted to her although many important questions bothered him. *Was this really a true love? Was he drawing something from Emily that met the neediness he felt in his life? Was it just loneliness that drew him to Emily?*

Fears that he had not fully grappled with, surfaced as he thought about the relationship failure of his own parents and the emptiness he felt towards his father. Grayson wondered how he could make a relationship work in a sustainable way if he was to marry her. *Would he be able to be a good husband to this beautiful young woman?* Financially he was reasonably secure with the balance of the Sutcliffe property sale still coming to him for a couple more years, not to mention the modest salary he earned from his work at the Museum. But providing practically was only one factor and Grayson possessed sufficient self-awareness to know that he had issues within himself that could present obstacles and introduce difficulty for him in emotionally nurturing a marriage partner.

The appointed time for Grayson to meet Emily's parents came. It had been many years since there had been any contact of course but Mr. Barker still had recollections of Grayson as the young boy that the schoolmaster had abused. Somehow he felt a cautious resistance to Grayson. As much as he tried to approach the prospective relationship without prejudice or reservation, he felt concerns that he could not shake.

Could it be possible that the boy he had known might have emerged into young manhood to become a strong and fitting partner and husband to his daughter? Mr. Barker had been unequivocal in making known such feelings about Grayson and it had been a source of contention between him and Emily. She resented her father's dogmatism and the way in which he expressed his views in no uncertain terms. Wanting to believe the best about Grayson, she confidently asserted that she could mend him and make up for any deficiency in the young man whom she claimed to now love. There was much in Grayson to love and Emily held fast to the notion that "love would conquer everything…"

Her ideals were noble but such idealism at this stage left much about their relationship that would remain unexplored and untested because of her tendency to gloss over things that Grayson internalized. Emily's optimism would in time prove to be misplaced and she would have cause to plead for Grayson to share his life more openly with her as she became more thoroughly acquainted with the broken and damaged elements of his life.

The evening began an hour or two before suppertime, when Grayson was introduced to Emily's folks in the hotel where the parents had come to stay. Their back country sheep station had prospered and with wool exports thriving, Emily's family had done well materially.

There were of course the expected exchanges and pleasantries during the meal and Grayson endured this as best he could. He was clearly nervous and on edge about whether or not the impression he was creating might be favorable.

Mr. Barker remembered Grayson as a shy little boy from the old school and he had been a strong advocate for uncovering the truth about the children's teacher, Mr. Pickett. Emily's father was a strong, assertive man prone to be somewhat blunt and artless in his domineering presence. He conducted an embarrassing monologue and appeared to have more interest in appraising Grayson of his own life than learning very much about any progress his daughter's young suitor might have made.

Since he had already made up his mind about Grayson and would not soften easily, he saw little point in entering into much dialogue. Emily's mother salvaged something from the night by inviting Grayson to tell them a "little about himself." This was something Grayson did in a very compelling and rather endearing manner. His story certainly evoked a measure of empathy when told—not that there was any contrivance on Grayson's part to elicit pity. In point of fact it was quite moving to hear him recount the nature of how he came to be forced into an unexpected departure from England and his subsequent arrival in New Zealand, his friendship and subsequent loss of dear friend Thomas, and his brave effort to carve out a life for himself there in the city of Christchurch. Understandably, any account of the episode at school with Mr. Pickett was noticeably absent.

Towards the end of the evening, Grayson respectfully asked Emily's parents permission for him to court their daughter. This was a request that the obnoxious Mr. Barker responded to with a broad sweep of his hand in Emily's direction.

"Well… I have to say I have my grave concerns which I have been frank about with my daughter…nevertheless Emily's sensible enough and if she sees something in you I will endeavor to trust her instincts and not make my opposition a stumbling block to you entering into courtship. But allow me to register my misgivings and may they be assuaged with time and the opportunity for becoming better acquainted with you."

"Father!" Emily exclaimed, "Do you know how condescending and patronizing you sound? Grayson is certainly someone that anybody could see *"something"* in if they just took the opportunity to listen and observe!"

It was subtle carp at her father for monopolizing the evening—a reality Mr. Barker would in all likelihood have been oblivious to. Emily was well used to her father's domineering manner and inclination to pomposity but in this instance she became enflamed and reacted with anger to his controlling, overbearing manner. Nonetheless, he arose seemingly unfazed from his chair and stretched across to grasp Grayson's hand and shake it firmly.

"Well my boy, glad to have met you again anyway and appreciate you having the decency to present yourself. All the very best for both of you."

With that he pecked his daughter lightly on the cheek and announced that he was ready to retire for the evening. It was an odd encounter.

Grayson walked Emily home through darkened streets with little being exchanged between them. Grayson appeared lost in his own thoughts. He was neither sullen or moody, just "somewhere else." It was a cloudy night with a light breeze that parted the clouds occasionally at which point moonlight seized the opportunity to burst through the gaps. Emily wished for at least some level of talk about how they felt the evening had gone and perhaps some romantic talk about what their future might look like. Yet Grayson who had years of practice and was adept at internalizing his deepest thoughts, was ominously silent.

While Grayson felt he loved Emily, he wasn't so sure he was worth being loved in return. This was a very real issue for him. His past had produced the misbelief that he was somehow unworthy of being loved. He found himself locked up with feelings that could not be released and emotions that were all stifled.

Grayson thought that what he felt for Emily was love, but grappled with the question that if he loved her, shouldn't he let her find someone better? The self-doubt and the inner shame he carried seemed to rest on his shoulders like a heavy cloak. It made it so difficult to actually receive love and in turn express love. Here in the light of the moon, its full reflection caught her face every so often as they walked. Emily looked especially lovely.

"Sorry it was not a very easy night for you. Did you hate them so very badly?"

"The evening was fine and so are your parents. I'm just thinking about how you deserve the very best Emily," Grayson murmured softly.

She slipped her arm in under his, walking closely by his side.

"I think I've found the very best," said Emily squeezing his arm affectionately in response.

She wasn't completely sure, but it occurred to her that looking up into Grayson's face in the moonlight, that tears sparkled in his eyes.

"I wish I could believe that," he said, his voice breaking. "Am I really good for you Emily…can you really see yourself being happy with me?"

The self-loathing sense of shame and personal inadequacy Grayson carried, seemed to rob him of joyfully accepting that he was loved for who he was and that *he* was the person who actually carried the potential to make Emily very happy. To her, in spite of his uncertainties about himself, Grayson was a kind, thoughtful young man who was intelligent, and interesting, standing out far and beyond others she knew of. For Emily the deal was done. She wanted Grayson to talk about their marriage and share the dreams he had of his life together with her.

Grayson felt awkward and struggled to talk about his personal dreams and longings…he had plenty he could share that had to do with doubts, fears and uncertainties, but he felt that was not what Emily was looking for at that moment.

Inwardly she longed for Grayson to take the lead and to open up some meaningful conversation from his heart about their growing love for she intuitively understood that such communication could assist in bringing a sense of strength and depth to their relationship.

It was true that Grayson had received poor modeling in the areas of responsibilities and roles within a healthy marriage but Emily felt confident she was right for Grayson and could love him out of himself. In her eyes, here was a decent young man whose life was damaged, but not beyond repair. She loved his winsome ways. In an ominous kind of way his lack of dominance was quite attractive and it was empowering for Emily.

Grayson was thinking about something his friend Thomas Sutcliffe had said. Tom had never married but he had some wisdom on the matter.

"It's more important to BE the right person in a marriage than it is to carry on worrying if you have found the right person. Too many people get married having looked for the "right person" to get married to and then fail to BE the right person once they are married..."

To Grayson it made sense, but could he *be* the right person for Emily? To *be* the right person you had to *behave* as the right person. Grayson had come to understand that his father had most likely not *been* the right person for his mother as demonstrated by the way he had apparently conducted himself. He often thought about his father's choices and the failure he had been as a husband and as a father.

Grayson realized that somehow a significant connection existed between his father's behavior and why he himself felt so "broken."

It was a formative factor in his life that he was not at all reconciled with and he had no idea what to do about it.

"I'm so unclear and so anxious about so many things in my life and the role I'm even supposed to play in life," he confided in a rare moment of transparency as he walked in the moonlight with Emily.

"You're thinking way too much, that's all!" she laughingly teased, dismissing the dreadful inner turmoil that stirred in this young man and unwittingly short-circuiting the very conversation she had wanted to have. Emily's own sense of confidence and buoyancy had caused her to trivialize the issues Grayson struggled to find language for and shut him down as he took the risk of trying to articulate his feelings. He had briefly brought his strategy of avoidance to the surface and it had fleetingly been exposed...but now the moment and the opportunity had slipped away...once more.

With the passing of years, Grayson had used *avoidance* to survive but it was not in any sense, a useful survival strategy. For example, he *still* continued to find it too difficult to yet read his father's little leather notebook that Sutcliffe had passed onto him as they first left England. Grayson seemed to hold some vague comprehension of his father's brokenness and agonies, but resisted any direct confrontation with such knowledge, being fearful that it might amplify his own acute sense of being *dis-ordered.*

Becoming acquainted with details about his father's life terrified Grayson. It failed to dawn on him that anything he could ever discover might actually help him and provide the mirror that he needed in order to find personal, inner wholeness. Part of him wanted to read the messages his father had recorded but he always "stalled" at the critical point.

Perhaps he should read the journal tonight? Maybe when he got back after seeing Emily safely home he should take the time to open the little brown leather suitcase and read the carefully stored, unread words that his father had penned long ago.

But then...if he *didn't*, it could always keep for another time he reasoned.

11

BROKEN FATHER, BROKEN FAMILY

Like many couples, Grayson and Emily were to discover that after the wedding comes a marriage. Early on, some misunderstandings and difficulties confirmed the reality that marriages aren't made in heaven but right here on earth with hard work and application.

It had been a traditional wedding with the small chapel overflowing with guests and well wishers who then enjoyed a delightful reception with a roasted lamb dinner at the Barker family's country estate. Grayson had felt an acute sense of shame that he had no family with him to share the day. How he wished that Thomas had still been alive to witness the occasion.

With the wedding behind them Grayson and Emily rented a little dwelling in the city. He continued his work with the Museum and she continued to paint and work on her commissions. Emily was a born homemaker. Putting her artistic flair to good use she made their little home comfortable and attractive. She had the ability to transform things that were bland and uninteresting into items that were cheerful and vibrant. She had a remarkable eye for turning mundane caste-offs that others might not see any potential in, into delightful as well as functional items around their home with a little concentrated thought and effort. The pity was that this talent for bringing additional vitality to things she collected did not appear to include Grayson within its scope particularly. Emily's greatest assignment and challenge as she saw it, lay not in transforming her environment as much as it did in trying to change her husband.

The attributes that Grayson had displayed initially had been part of what was an attraction for Emily, but now at times instead of seeing them as strengths, those same characteristics became a source of great irritation to her. He was still much the same person—gentle, quietly reflective and not given to being verbose. Emily at times struggled to draw leadership from Grayson or to elicit opinions and personal feelings from her husband.

To Emily it seemed Grayson was unappreciative and failed to notice her efforts. Grayson was a decent person and certainly noticed with gratitude, his young wife's input but for him to be expressive and demonstrative did not come easily. It seemed to Emily that he would just shut down and slip into deep reflective quiet spells that she interpreted as being morose. She would feel at times as if his apparent lack of appreciation equated to his disapproval of her although this was certainly not the case. He was capable of great warmth but his quiet reflectiveness and shy personality were traits that often produced the effect of him being perceived by Emily and others as sullen. Emily generally maintained hope beyond these difficulties, believing that her own personality would be enough to undo the areas where due to his background, Grayson showed caution and reserve.

Apart from the time in his life that Grayson had shared with Thomas, relating well at a close level was not something he had ever had opportunity to become strong in.

Grayson loved Emily and wanted to please her and be acceptable but battled the relentless feeling that he was continually failing. At times he would try to converse meaningfully with her instead of following a kind of instinct to want to retreat inwardly or to bury himself in an interesting book. He was fully aware that with raised eyebrows people might express under their breath sentiments such as, *"What on earth did she see in him?"*

Those types of comments would filter back to the young couple and it hurt them both deeply. The way Grayson happened to be, haunted him at times and he was an ongoing mystery to himself. He very much wanted to be admired by Emily and not to be under her shadow.

There were times when out of desperation, Grayson wondered if he tried to talk to God in the same way he had heard Thomas do it, if anything might happen. Sadly he made the mistake of feeling a little like someone who needed an introduction first. Even though he wanted the intimacy that Tom seemed to have with God, Grayson found himself strangely resistant to act on the words Tom had gasped as he was dying or the gentle urging Tom had encouraged upon Grayson in the letter he had left in the wooden chest.

At their wedding ceremony the vicar had said marriage was God's idea and that Grayson and Emily were getting married *in the sight of God.* It was acceptable enough to know that God was watching, but allowing Him to get too close and fully trusting Him seemed like narrowing down the options a bit and losing independence. The most unfortunate thing was that they both failed to understand that was exactly what they both needed to do, and that it could have changed everything.

Both Grayson and Emily took their marriage and the vows they had made to each other seriously. But they soldiered on without either of them ever personally and purposefully requesting God's intervention in their lives or in their marriage. It was like leaving a gentle, kindly Stranger outside and unacquainted, while He knocked on the door holding every one of the keys vital to their life's success and fulfillment.

In June 1871 Grayson and Emily became the proud parents of a baby boy. Little Joseph Thomas Pollock was born to a father who had long held misgivings about his capability to be a good Daddy. The moment Grayson held this little son in his arms he felt incredible emotions of tenderness and of overwhelming responsibility. But the old fears were there in force too, causing him to question both his worth and suitability for the task.

For Emily, motherhood was something she was ready for and the increased demand on her time and diminished personal time for painting did not bother her. She gave herself to the role of parenting in a way that Grayson found difficult to emulate. While little Joseph was so small and was being nursed, Grayson felt somewhat redundant. He didn't want to feel that way, but his lack of success in pacifying their little one tended to reinforce his sense of merely being a somewhat superfluous bystander. And of course Emily was so capable, highlighting the sense of awkwardness he felt.

In a generation when there was little freedom in talking about family roles and relationships and much was left to assumption, Grayson languished in the shadows ignorant of the importance of offering a supportive presence from the outset for his son's life. Grayson believed his role would only really begin once the child had grown a little and a meaningful connection could take place. That was a sad mistake because it begged the question of just how old would the child be before this "meaningful connection" would occur? Would the distance created and his aloof fathering style end up becoming a habit?

City life for the new family was not altogether easy from a practical point of view, apart from the adjustments they were making together. By 1876 the city of Christchurch had a population of over 12,000 in the central city and another 10,000 in the suburbs. The increase in the number of people living in the city during the mid 1870's led to serious health problems with epidemics of diphtheria and whooping cough. Worse however was the typhoid outbreak that claimed many lives. The waste of the city ran into the Avon River with kitchen waste and chamber pots being emptied into channels running along the sides of the streets. Manure from the animals that provided the transport in the city just added to the problem.

Joseph was barely five years old when he became seriously ill. His distraught parents sought medical intervention that at the time was under considerable stress with the demands of hundreds being unwell and deaths happening frequently. Joseph improved in time, but his delicate health caused the family to make the decision to withdraw from city life for a while and to shift out to live in the country on the sprawling farm estate of Emily's parents, the Barkers. The move was motivated by all the right reasons but with the passage of time, the wisdom of this young family becoming intensely integrated into the ordered social structure of Emily's father's household could be deemed to be questionable. It was a tightly knitted working community of people where clearly you either fitted the culture and fully imbibed the values and interests of a big sheep station—or you simply didn't.

Grayson did his best but found little opportunity to prove himself and be accepted as a useful contributor to those he felt were his assessors. So it was, when a more fitting opportunity presented itself, Grayson found it justifiable and of some relief to secure another avenue of meaningful employment.

He secured some tutoring work in a nearby country school with a small roll of about twenty children ranging from six to thirteen years of age. Working with one other teacher he found fresh challenge in that position and put effort into trying to be approachable with his young charges as well as making his lessons interesting and engaging. His own love for learning and the wide spread of knowledge he had accumulated meant Grayson was well appreciated even though he won no prizes for being the most socially skilled schoolmaster that ever graced the teaching profession.

The introduction of compulsory schooling for children in 1877 had significant impact upon children living in rural areas. This regulation reduced the level of their input into farm work, although it took some time before school attendance was consistent or regular for many pupils, particularly at harvest times. Grayson took teaching seriously and even though he did not see this as a career path nor planned to be in this post for too long, he approached it wholeheartedly.

Months scrolled by and as they did, a subtle change began to take place within the family. In the process of time things grew tense and then...sour.

What was intended to be a temporary stay at the Barker property lasting for an unspecified time stretched out, first to one year and then another. Grayson was alarmed at the way he felt undermined in this place as Emily's husband and the father of little Joseph, now almost seven years old. But he was too paralyzed to do anything about it even though he could see this disturbing trend happening on an almost daily basis.

In his deferential manner Grayson found himself retreating into a private isolated world and although it was not an intentional strategy, it became a coping mechanism to remain where he felt safe. It was as if from there, life was manageable. Avoidance became survival but inevitably it would force a crisis.

Grayson's parents in law and extended family slowly but surely assumed some of the roles that a father would naturally be inclined towards. Emily's parents were good grandparents in many respects and Grayson imagined himself being supplanted often by their competence and dominance. It wasn't something they contrived, it just happened and to Grayson's disappointment Emily seemed quite relaxed, even abetting the situation and appeared indignant when he proposed moving back into the city.

Grayson loved Joseph but felt like he was in a competition he could never win with doting grandparents and a busy household providing plenty to keep a little boy active and interested. He found himself withdrawing further from Joseph and the other family members. Even from Emily. The worst part about things from his viewpoint was that she barely seemed to notice or if she had, lacked the concern to rectify what was happening.

It terrified him as he saw that somehow an old family *dynamic* was occurring before his very eyes. A cycle was perpetuating in a way that he felt powerless to alter as if it was pre-ordained and almost propelled by forces outside of his control.

One evening Grayson planned an opportunity to talk with his wife. It was a good plan but it didn't go well at all. Grayson pled with Emily to make arrangements to pack up with Joseph and to accompany him as they made their return to the city. Sadly Grayson's entreaty unintentionally conveyed more about what he felt was important for him over and above any other factor. His reasoning was not clear to Emily neither was the sense of urgency that constrained her husband. It appeared more to her to be a direct statement of jealousy against her family. Nonetheless, she said she loved him and wanted to do what was best for *them* but would negotiate a move on the basis that it would take at least another month or two to prepare for the shift back to the city. She gave him license to even go immediately if that was what he really wanted and to find a teaching job and a home for them. At that point she would return.

So it was, that one week later Grayson packed some belongings and returned to Christchurch on his own.

It was quite a different place to the city he had left over two years ago. By 1879 there were more people, many new buildings, a new railway system and importantly, expensive iron pipes had been imported to facilitate the building of a system of sewers in the central city. The building of the city cathedral that had faltered when money ran out once the foundations had been laid back in 1865 had later been re-commenced and by the time Grayson had arrived back, the tower and main part of the Cathedral were starting to take shape.

The new Normal School had opened in Cranmer Square and become New Zealand's first teachers' training college. It was there Grayson was to secure employment. His work in the museum, his training, in particular his love of literature and then two years in a country school equipped him well to spread his time between teaching pupils as well as some responsibilities in training future teachers.

Grayson spent some time looking for suitable accommodation for Emily and Joseph to come and join him soon. He found simple lodgings for himself within walking distance of his work and then proceeded to look for a suitable home for his family. He became busy with his work and it was harder than anticipated to find a suitable place to bring Emily and Joseph back to. Actually it was more bothersome to him than it was difficult.

A month slipped by and he wrote to Emily to say he had work but was still looking for a home. He hoped it would not take too long, stating he wanted them to be together as soon as possible.

Another month slipped by followed by yet another. Grayson was finding a good deal of satisfaction in his work and it was this that dulled any real sense of isolation from his wife and child. He thought of them and missed them of course but his work and the preparation it entailed, prevented him from feeling too great a sense of distress.

Meanwhile Emily waited. She longed for a passionate pursuit from Grayson that might give an indication of fervency on his part. To her it seemed their relationship was in a precarious place with her husband evidently displaying a take it or leave it stance in contending for them to be re-united. This was a position she could not tolerate because of the uncertainty it conveyed. It was precisely part of the reason why she had insisted on needing a little time before she would move back to Christchurch. She had hoped it would be the testing and proving of something between them…but it was not playing out in a way that she found encouraging.

12

THE CHASM WIDENS

It was over six months before Grayson found a little house in the suburbs that he decided he could buy with money from Thomas Sutcliffe's estate, some savings he had put aside and a very small loan to make up the balance. The smallish, ageing house was plain and situated on a large sloping front paddock backing onto a bush reserve with trees and shrubs that formed a pleasant backdrop. It had a wide gable end with a window centered in the middle opening out from an upstairs attic area. A pleasant verandah ran the length of the frontal aspect of the house. A chimney exited the roof from inside the lounge where there was a brick fireplace that offered both an attractive feature as well as a practical necessity for the cold winters.

He was sure Emily would love the house and apply her skills to making up for its somewhat bland appearance. He wrote to her excitedly and explained what he had done and how the house would thrive with her touch. He was sure she would be proud of him for taking initiative and providing them with a home...in spite of the time it had taken.

He posted the letter off with a great sense of optimism and believed a change was imminent for his family.

But it would not be the change he had hoped for and waited for expectantly. A letter came back in due course from Emily which seemed strangely detached and scarcely made mention of the house he had purchased or other matters he had raised. Naturally this was far from what Grayson had hoped for and it created profound disappointment. Emily's apparent trivializing of the matters that were foremost on Grayson's mind was partially understandable in that Joseph had been unwell again and Emily was putting aside any plans to move into the city with Grayson for an undetermined time until the child had fully recovered. It was a cruel blow.

At the earliest opportunity, during a holiday period, Grayson took the trip out to the Barker's property to be with his wife and his son Joseph.

"Come to your Dadda Joseph!"

Grayson had called out hoping for a responsive welcome as he walked up the long tree-lined driveway, duffle bag in hand. He had spotted his little boy hanging off a fence only a stone's throw away watching some men working with a flock of sheep corralled into a small pen. While it was re-assuring for Grayson to see his son had recovered from illness sufficiently to be up and about, it hurt him that Joseph found greater interest in what he was watching than the fact that his father had just arrived.

He barely acknowledged his wounded father who was left feeling as if he was vying for his son's attention. Hesitating, uncertain whether to join the group or to carry on up to the house, Grayson chose to continue to make his way up to the homestead where he hoped he might find Emily.

The men cringed, knowing it would seem like a slight and ventured to offer a hearty "hello" and a friendly compensatory wave as their gesture of goodwill. For Grayson that all too familiar feeling of being excluded that he recognized he had lived with from childhood…the sense of always being out of place, flooded through his being again. That lurking, dark shadow subjecting him to thoughts and feelings of being like an outsider had "ridden" on his emotions since he was a little boy and it still caused him to dread company for the fear of being rejected. At heart, it was this emotion that pre-disposed

Grayson to dysfunctional behavior in every personal relationship and even conditioned how he approached life in general. He resisted the strong temptation to turn around immediately and return to the city realizing he should make the effort to oppose such emotions—as hard as it was to do so.

Joseph loved the farm life with its routines, the familiar smells of a sheep station and all that went with country living. The boy had reason to feel a sense of resistance and suspicion about his father's arrival at the farm. Emily had told Joseph that they would be going back to the city with his father and that he would be coming to get them at some point. She had not deliberately planned to paint such a move in a negative light but Joseph had certainly begun to view it in such a way.

"Some day your father will be coming to take us to the new house he has bought in the big city darling," she had reminded him on a number of occasions.

"I don't think Dadda loves me if he wants to come here and to take me away."

"Of course he loves you. You're his only little boy and he wants you to be where he is."

"But why does he want me to be with him when he's busy and he doesn't do anything with me even when he is here ?"

It was a point Emily found hard to defend.

Hours later, after Grayson's arrival, the little boy gave his father a hug with encouragement to do so, but it grieved him that his boy seemed to have frozen him out. Grayson felt confirmation of this was evidenced by the lack of relish his son held for the simplest of physical gestures...a hug, sitting on his knee...anything.

Joseph exhibited almost no level of enthusiasm at all that his father had returned for a while.

This insecure father could not see such a reaction might be a normal outflow of the simple reality that he had not been around for a time. In a child's perception, a six-month absence was forever. With thoughtful application, and by taking appropriate steps to mend the stilted relationship, things could have in all likelihood thawed. A child such as Joseph might have readily opened his heart to a father expressing delight just to be with his son in natural, spontaneous ways.

But Grayson did not seem to find the resources within himself to intuitively know where to start and what to do.

A resilient father with good self esteem and perseverance would have doggedly and relentlessly given time and effort to bonding with his son. It should have been a most natural process. But gnawing inside Grayson was the inability he struggled with, to display genuine affection for his son in an outward way without it being a perfunctory mechanical response. Tragically, it was not a natural thing to do for this father who was reproducing exactly the same dynamic he had experienced with his own father, who yet again had not experienced a loving relationship, with *his* father.

Grayson glibly put it down to being a "Pollock thing" and tried to forget the ache he had experienced in his own soul, when as a child he had longed for his father's love and affirmation. A reality he knew had damaged him and impaired his own ability to now relate well with Joseph. He also feared the disintegration that had been occurring in his marriage as well and reflected on what he knew of the collapse of his parents' relationship.

It was true and Grayson recognized the difficulty between fathers and sons in the Pollock family was being visited again, together with a marriage that was failing and he had no clue where to start rebuilding. Grayson seemed to be under the influence of a malevolent, destructive force that deceived him into believing the falsehood that a future with Emily and Joseph had become too much of a mountain to even tackle.

Such thinking was of itself, to become self-fulfilling.

Being back in close proximity to Emily and Joseph should have helped but if anything it made things worse for Grayson. He felt a chasm had opened up between him and Joseph that he was powerless to bridge. Almost certainly this would *not* have been the case but because it seemed to be the reality, it *became* the reality as Grayson withdrew instead of pressing in and forging a bond with his son.

Emily and Joseph were naturally enough very close and it emphasized to Grayson the gap that he was allowing to develop in the role he owned, as a father to his son. Joseph was a curious little boy who had become accustomed to an outdoor lifestyle and the many interesting aspects it offered. His interest in the farm animals extended to virtually any creature at all, from the birdlife to small creepy crawly insect life. Joseph's curiosity led him to follow his grandfather around like a shadow and he loved to sit in front of him as they rode on horseback over the sizeable farm property. He would don his grandfather's hat and saunter around like the lord of the manor. Being the first and only grandson, Joseph indeed had a special place.

What Grayson failed to accept, is that he too had a special place that nobody else in the world could ever fulfill. Joseph needed a father who was present both physically as well as at an emotionally nurturing level. It could have been his for the taking, but like his father before him, he found himself empty inside, abdicating and estranging himself from his son.

This situation tore at Emily. She saw Grayson's impotence in urgently seeking to repair his family relationships as passivity and did not comprehend the inner turmoil and frustrated agonies her husband experienced. Emily had come to believe that Joseph could continue to find enjoyment and improved health in this rural setting among her family, while a nagging sense of guilt told her that she should be alongside her husband in the city. Until things changed, she preferred to use Joseph's health as an excuse for not shifting back to Christchurch. Emily had few doubts that Grayson loved his little son and her for that matter too, but marveled at the blank, resignation he appeared to have for doing little to fight to salvage the quality of their family life.

The time came for Grayson to end the visit after a week and he packed his belongings, heavy-hearted and despondent. He needed to return for the commencement of another term and surprisingly was leaving, still with an unclear picture of what he believed Emily actually needed as far as their marriage was concerned. Compounding that reality was the fact that as well, he had no idea as to how he could ever change and be different in his role as a husband and father.

Grayson failed to see the enormity of the negative contribution he personally had introduced into his marriage, tending to underplay the correlation between the display of Emily's reserved lack of warmth, and his own behaviors.

Emily had tried so often to be warm and encouraging but now wearied of her husband's lack of consistency and introverted, awkward ways. Grayson failed to understand why it was that he produced the exasperated reactions in his wife that left him feeling barely tolerated. His occasional attempts to overcome his default setting for being distant by showing a little affection, were wooden and lacked spontaneity. Inevitably his earnest yet clumsy approaches would be untimely and they were shrugged off. Emily was warily protecting herself from having her hopes raised, then being disappointed by a husband who was unpredictable and seemed incapable of lasting change.

Grayson had recollections as a child of seeing his father being rejected by his mother. He'd wondered why his mother rebuffed his father at the time. When he was older he had gained a greater measure of understanding regarding his father's infidelity. He'd wondered about the possibilities of what might have caused his mother's reactions to make her so distant. He was unsure whether his mother's responses had been *because* of his father's behavior or if her reactions had been the catalyst that promoted his father's pursuit of another relationship.

Now with Grayson struggling to grasp Emily's lack of response to him, he came to the conclusion that since his failures were not of the magnitude of his father, that she might be at fault and playing a part in creating his problems. He reasoned that any case Emily had against him was surely insufficient for her to feel so aggrieved with him.

Emily had begun her marriage full of expectation and given herself in every way she knew to help inspire Grayson to being the man she felt he could be. It was a relentless, repetitive pattern. Now despairing after years of trying, she felt she had nothing left to give unless certain changes were to be initiated from her husband that should give her reason to hope. She found her inclination to keep hoping Grayson could ever truly be different had waned.

Feeling incapable of changing and fearful of ever being different, his only instinct was to withdraw. It was a pathetic impasse.

Grayson arrived back in Christchurch with emptiness inside him that he had no idea how to fill. Settling into the house he had purchased for Emily and Joseph, he was uncertain as to how the future would unfold, lacking any clarity about whether or not his wife and son would ever join him. It seemed like they were slipping away from his reach and he began to adopt a victim mentality rather than appreciating the ways in which he had contributed to the situation he now faced.

Without understanding and failing to fully recognize his contribution, he would never be in a position to be different and to bring about the changes needed. The changes that were *needed* and the changes that were to come about were two very different matters.

Sadly what developed next, never needed to happen.

It could have been different and the erosion between a couple as well as a father and son was entirely preventable. Yet permission was granted for an old family curse to stealthily creep up on them and wreck havoc through lack of vigilant defending and guarding their love for one another. The lie that it was inevitable for families in the Pollock line to disintegrate was yet again being accepted and as a result would be once more be perpetuated.

Grayson's place of employment along with books and learning now became the environment where he began to bury himself and where he sought to draw his life and identity from. He was like a person dying of thirst, searching for water and digging a *well*—in fact he dug one well after another for himself only to find none of them ever truly satisfied his inner longings. Feeling personal failure in life at many levels, in his own inner world, with his marriage and with his family, caused him to dig yet another well as he sought satisfaction by gaining the approval of others in his work setting. Grayson's cravings were completely normal and understandable but the issue was that where he sought to have those needs met was misplaced—each time he dug a new "well" it would at best, only ever be a leaky substitute for the encounter he really needed…an encounter with *Someone* who was there for him all along. Such an encounter was pivotal and could transform everything. Until then, no amount of "digging" would ever yield the purpose and meaning Grayson had always longed for in his life.

The desperate search for personal identity and significance continually found him looking to *something* for the meeting of his needs and to provide a cure for the sense of lack he felt as a person. Searching in wrong directions inevitably ended in cold, bleak disappointment and led to further introversion and consolidation of all Grayson's failures and fears. His deepest desires were entirely valid but they would never be satisfied without the *"Encounter"* he needed and the life-giving transformation this could bring.

For Grayson the tragedy was…what might have been.

13

AN AWKWARD INTRODUCTION

Loud knocking broke the dusky silence and stirred Grayson from lightly dozing in the armchair at the fireside.

Blinking into reality he looked at the clock and wondered where time had gone. The fire he had lit to keep warm several hours before in the afternoon, had burned to a few glowing embers in the grate. He coughed. It was a persistent cough that wracked his whole body and it had bothered him for months.

Who could be at the door he wondered? It wasn't like he had visitors who came with any frequency at all and the doctor would never make house calls this late in the evening.

The knocking persisted as he lifted himself out of the Chesterfield and made his way, coughing, to the door. The place was unkempt and had become run-down. More so than he could ever have realized. Even with half an objective eye to see the true state of his living conditions, Grayson would have been appropriately embarrassed. It was late August 1896 and the tidy little house Grayson had purchased those many years ago had deteriorated in the care of a man who had lost his way in life.

Here was a man who had become accustomed to his own company and although he was not completely oblivious to the state of his surroundings, he had ceased to care.

Unlocking the door Grayson peered cautiously into the cold evening air to see a young man and a young woman on the bottom step huddled together for a bit of warmth. The young man walked back up to the top step.

Still coughing, Grayson squinted intensely at him wondering who this visitor could be and what purpose he had knocking on his door.

"Hello Dad," the young man said quietly, extending his hand.

"Joseph?" Grayson enquired wistfully. "Is this you Joseph?"

It had been seventeen years since father and son had had any personal face to face contact…seventeen years since Grayson had returned to his work in Christchurch and become immersed in a life of academic introversion. Yes, there had been written contact between Grayson and Emily and a little with Joseph, gifts being sent on occasion, but with the passing of years, so too had passed anything meaningful in terms of this family's relationship—it had just had faded. It was a tragic and unnecessary outcome that need never have been allowed to develop.

Emily had waited for some hint of anything that might give her assurance that Grayson was going to rise to becoming the husband that she needed him to be, but he seemed bound and inextricably locked up in his own internal world of uncertainty, shame and insecurity. He recognized that there was a part of him that deeply wanted Emily to return and be with him in Christchurch with their young son while at the same time, another part seemed to persuade him into believing that they would probably be better off without him. He had even expressed this in a letter to Emily which tended to reinforce to her the impression that Grayson was too emotionally disabled to stand up and "fight" for his wife and family.

The purchase of the house for them to live in as a family, had momentarily given rise to a little hope for Emily but it had stalled at that point when Grayson seemed passionless and unwilling to ardently pursue things to the next stage. Understandably Emily held concerns about the display of such passivity and feared any prospect of exchanging the security and stability of her parent's family home for the prospect of a life of uncertainty with her seemingly diffident husband.

"Yes, it's me father..." said the young man expressionlessly.

"Come, come in...please come inside..." stammered Grayson huskily as he reached out his arm in a beckoning motion. The couple stepped off the verandah and entered into the little house to stand awkwardly as Grayson shuffled papers and other household items out of the way to clear a place for them to sit. Grayson's outer world reflected his inner world to a significant degree. His home was in a state of disrepair—untidy, not very clean, uninviting and cluttered with books and papers and a scattering of unwashed dishes. There was nothing very appealing there.

Looking around the disorderly room, Joseph felt a strange alienation from the nervous man who sat opposite him with anxious expectation written on his face. He found himself feeling slightly disdainful, but surprisingly, at that moment not despising this man who was his father—nor did he feel any particular flicker of warmth or bond either. Just neutral...it was like trying to be pleasant to a stranger he thought inwardly.

"I'm not staying," said Joseph in a matter of fact way... "I've come to introduce you to Sarah."

Having already taken a seat, the young lady half stood and stretched forward to shake Grayson's hand. He was also on his feet, nervously wiping the hand he had been covering his mouth with while coughing, on his trouser leg as the introduction was taking place.

"Very pleased to meet you Sarah," Grayson croakily said.

"Sarah and I are getting married in three weeks time and we felt it was the courteous thing to let you know and invite you should you wish to come."

Grayson could probably never have comprehended the agonies this young couple had gone through in coming to agreement to take the time to visit Joseph's father and extend this invitation. Together they had wrestled with the issue of eliminating Grayson from their lives entirely or at least giving him an opportunity to show some level of interest and connection. Emily held only the slightest interest in seeing Grayson and had not particularly relished the idea of him being present at their son's wedding to this lovely young lady. But that was selfish and she released her son and future daughter in law to do what they felt they needed to do.

Over his nearly twenty-six years, Joseph really had received so little contact or input from his father, that he felt he owed him nothing. True, there was some underlying resentment even cynicism, but in this moment there was no accusation being leveled at this father by his son. Grayson of course knew and felt his own failure deeply, instinctively knowing that he had been like his father before him—actually it was something Grayson had often pondered…why did he feel an instinct to back away when it would have been the right instinct to pursue relationship with his flesh and blood? It was that same dark, familiar brokenness that dogged the marriages and family life of the Pollock line.

Without intending to Grayson had duplicated with his own wife and son, the very dynamic he himself had experienced with *his* father. In spite of promising himself that he would try to be different, the fact was, Joseph now stood before him as living proof that Grayson had failed, under different circumstances, but failed nonetheless every bit as much as he had felt his own father had failed him.

Inside he ached for the damage he knew he would have caused this young man who now stood before him. He knew the wounds and complexities his son would carry and in this moment Grayson wanted to reach out to him. He wanted to offer some sort of signal to this boy who he had never adequately parented. He had never sought to fail his son—neither had he ever intended to be an utterly ineffective father. After all, he knew so well firsthand how a little boy craved for his Daddy's love. He was ashamed and so very sorry that he had been an impotent, absent father who had failed in almost every conceivable respect. Grayson expected to be utterly rejected by his son but might this visit perhaps suggest otherwise?

Sarah was an attractive young woman. Stylish and tall, she had long dark hair falling easily to the sides of her face. Her hair framed finely chiseled cheek-bones as it cascaded down around her shoulders, resting naturally and easily about the collar of a stylish hounds tooth coat she was wearing. Joseph helped her take the garment off and dusting the back of a chair, again somewhat disdainfully, he laid it down carefully. Sarah was wearing what appeared to be beautifully tailored clothing. She gave evidence to have come from a privileged family background yet her refinement and elegance however did not communicate anything of aloofness. Grayson observed her cautiously feeling a little conscious of his disheveled state. He had cause to feel ruffled, as not only was this visit a complete surprise but he possessed sufficient self-awareness to imagine correctly that his appearance was likely to be worse than he comprehended. Yet Sarah gave no indication of being uneasy. Actually, if the truth was to be known, it was her that had coaxed and reasoned with Joseph to overcome his profound reluctance to even enter his father's dwelling. The part she had played influencing Joseph to seek this opportunity to meet with his father, hinted at substance of maturity and character that ran deeper than mere physical beauty.

Together she and Joseph had talked about "foundations" to marriage and how the things each partner brought into the union, inevitably shaped for good or bad, the way their lives would be built together. She was astute enough to know Joseph could not possibly be left unscathed by his family background and the legacy of disruption that was clearly evident. Joseph appeared less concerned than she was while conceding at a token level that he too wanted the basis of their union to be strong without underlying flaws that could jeopardize their happiness together.

Sarah had learned quite a bit about Joseph's father and had many questions about his story. In fact the learning of that story had unsettled her and made her slightly uneasy in her relationship with Joseph. Refusing to sweep history under the carpet, she had spoken often with the mother of her husband to be, Emily, and heard about the pain that Grayson had been through. In her mind she had wondered if that pain, had in turn been visited upon the next in the family line. Sarah had heard how Emily believed her love for Grayson would be enough to fix things and make it better. But it hadn't. And now she herself was in love with the son of a man with a dubious legacy she found herself having misgivings about...*just how "whole" was Joseph and might there be some unseen dynamic in this Pollock family that remained unresolved? And just what might it take to halt the negative influences of a generational line? Would her love for Joseph be enough to change things in a way that Emily's love had not changed Grayson?*

She had so many questions...certainly there was sufficient reason for her to feel concern about underlying unresolved issues which might have impacted upon the life of the man she loved and planned to marry. She was not so head over heels in love that she was blinded to understanding that any demons in Joseph's lineage had to have impact on her life too as his future wife.

"I've been looking forward to meeting you very much," ventured Sarah bravely.

She shot a glance at Joseph who in the poor light of the musty little lounge room was sitting there brooding, in stilted silence. Startled, she briefly imagined she saw a reflection of Grayson in Joseph and it caught her completely by surprise. Joseph was well dressed, always immaculately presented and in a physical sense bore little resemblance to his father. But just for a second it was like a *shadow* on both of these men that gave them the look of being out of the same "mold". It caused her to swallow hard as she struggled to regain composure in what was already a very awkward and tense situation—but Sarah ploughed on gamely.

"We'd love for you to come and be a part of our wedding...I'd like very much for you to get to know me," Sarah said flushing at the realization of the irony that this father had never even figured out how to get to know his own son, much less having the chance of ever getting to know the bride of that son.

After an hour of stilted small-talk Joseph stood to his feet. They'd covered some ground about Sarah's family, how they had met and where they might live but now Joseph had clearly enough. With one hand he beckoned for Sarah to prepare to leave while with the other he stretched over and shook his father's hand.

"We'd better get going. Hope you feel better soon. If you can come to the wedding it would say something about you wanting the best for our future."

With that, he picked up her coat, pointedly flicking off the dust and took Sarah by the hand, leading her to the door. Grayson followed. He was now balding and greying-old for his fifty-six years with a stooped posture that made him look even more aged than he actually was. His unkempt appearance and constant cough also made him seem older than his years and contributed to the impression of him perhaps being a somewhat unapproachable eccentric. If the truth was known, such a description was not particularly accurate. Grayson was shy but not unapproachable. Sadly, when someone is given a negative label they can tend to live down to those labels... and here was a man that few had ever really looked at long enough and hard enough to find the good. From childhood he had lived out of a damaged soul and the hurt in his life had transferred to others. When Grayson had lost Thomas Sutcliffe, all those years ago, he'd lost a person who really did believe in him.

For a while, Emily too had restored Grayson's self-belief but as his wife, she also needed to be nurtured and cherished. A man who feels so broken and inadequate, can never fully be a reliable support to others as his own neediness blinds him to seeing their needs—Emily could not take the burden of playing the relentless life-coach role for her husband without receiving the love and replenishment she needed in return.

Joseph and Sarah slipped out into the evening leaving Grayson lost in thought. Of course he should go to his son's wedding. Why would he not attend when they had extended a particular invitation to him? Feeling unwell was a lame excuse. While part of him wanted to go to the wedding he found himself inexplicably shying away from the idea—it seemed that the very thought of attending provoked every doubt and introverted fear to rise up and seize him deep inside. He could think of many compelling arguments why he should "just leave them be." Of course it was unreasonable, perhaps even irrational but emotional and spiritual brokenness causes foolish responses and it is never reasonable. This was a man who exemplified how it is that a person can carry wounds and brokenness from their family line and perpetuate them down the generations. Ignorance is never bliss. Sadly Grayson was ignorant of the evil dynamic being played out in his family. It was like a malevolent plot by an enemy to rob him of his destiny and destroy the wellbeing and family life of the Pollock line. Here was an assignment at work that had been originated by an evil force but perpetuated by flesh and blood…by poor choices and blindness to a scheme that operated with the aim of plundering the spiritual health and rob a family of their God-given destiny.

Slumped back in the rolled armed Chesterfield armchair, Grayson was breathing heavily with the rattle on his chest that he had become accustomed to. His mind scrolled over the years of his life. He felt deep remorse over the ways in which he had let his wife and son down. It was perplexing to him how in some respects he had been so much like his own father, a man he had never really known. He thought about the little brown leather suitcase he had brought out from England in 1850 as a nine-year-old. He thought of his mother putting the few little possessions he was taking for the trip into it. These were memories etched in his mind that readily triggered a recall of the emotions he felt at the time.

That same brown leather suitcase sat up in the attic, still containing the notebook that his father had wanted to be passed on to Grayson. It had remained unread all these years. Inexplicably, he had chosen to never read the contents in spite of the tearing desire to do so on a number of occasions. He'd decided to leave the disclosure of its pages to others.

Tears filled his eyes as he sat there in the gloom recalling the times he had spent with Thomas Sutcliffe. Grayson recalled the conversations he'd had with Thomas when he had spoken to him about the love that God had for him. Thomas had contrasted this with the fact that there really was a devil who was intent on destroying everything good that God had intended and planned for people. He had described how satan hated the things God loved-especially people and that humanity had meant so much to God, that He had provided a way of redemption.

Thomas had spoken about Jesus in a way a person would be inclined to talk about his best friend. The vicar who had presided at Grayson's wedding also hinted that a personal relationship with God was not only possible for anyone but it was necessary and the way he expressed it was similar to the letter Thomas had left in the chest. But Grayson had elected to continue as the "pilot" of his own ship, failing to see that this fundamental vote for self-governance lay at the heart of all his problems.

Thinking about his own wedding and the vicar's comments reminded him that he must decide what to do about Joseph and Sarah's wedding invitation.

Should he go to his son's wedding? He wrestled with the issue and finally out of the turmoil in his mind, a decision emerged.

Of course he should go.

The very next day Grayson filled out the little printed reply form to say he would be glad to come. Making his way out through the front door onto the verandah he cautiously walked over the wooden boards to the steps, proceeding from there down the incline across the straggly lawn to the street frontage. Coughing and hobbling along, he made his way to the little posting box down the street. The effort of a short walk took a big toll on him but he was glad he'd done it.

He would certainly attend his son's wedding and defeat any of the fears and misgivings he felt.

14

THE ABSENT WEDDING GUEST

Joseph had left his father's house with a sense of having laid down a challenge. He wanted his father to attend his wedding as some sort of statement that he at least cared a little bit. In a very small way it would go somewhere towards making amends.

Sarah and Joseph talked a lot about the meeting with Joseph's father. It was her influence that had been the driving factor in the meeting even happening. Left to Joseph it would most likely never have occurred. She saw some aspects of Joseph's personality and responses at times that bothered her slightly and was not naive enough to consider that the nature of his family life had not left a mark on him in some measure. Meeting Grayson had at least allowed Sarah to see a man who was not a monster—he was gentle, he was capable of being considerate but he was damaged by life and her interest to some extent lay in determining the level of impact this may have had on the man she planned to marry and spend her life with.

"I think your father has had a very sad life and is the way he is, because he feels rejected," Sarah commented. "He feels rejected and rejects himself—as well as always expecting others to," she continued.

"Well I could feel rejected by *him*," retorted Joseph. "I mean... to not seek an opportunity to see your son for seventeen years when it was possible by merely traveling a day or two!"

"He barely *ever* wrote or sent a gift...and if he had really wanted to, he could even have found somewhere to use a telephone," Joseph ranted. These were claims that it was difficult to refute—even the one about making a phone call was valid since in 1881, the first telephone exchange in New Zealand had opened in Christchurch—fifteen years previously.

"So there you have it ... my father showed by his actions how much he cared and what he really felt..."

"But if someone has suffered rejection then surely they are more likely to reject others?" questioned Sarah. "And it seems he was trying hard and very much wanting your mother and you to leave the farm and come to join him in Christchurch after he had bought the house," she gently countered.

Sarah was in love with Joseph—a handsome, talented man who had begun a promising career as an accountant. She was the daughter of a prominent lawyer in the city, with private school education and generally bore the cut of someone who had been born to a high society life-style, but gave no indication of seeing herself as a class apart from anyone else. Her father wanted the best for his daughter and saw Joseph as an ambitious young man who could provide well for her. Besides, Joseph had potential to become a person of note in the community and that mattered greatly to Sarah's father.

Sarah was a feisty young woman with opinions of her own. This was not a characteristic entirely approved of in woman, by the culture of the day. She saw in Joseph many good qualities but had to admit there were some niggling concerns that haunted her about Joseph. There was a slight aggressive edge that flared at times when Joseph was challenged or crossed. And there were the mood swings that took him into his own introverted world of silence at times. There were other observations too that Sarah generously discounted, accurately affirming that she "too had things to work on'" and that '"nobody is perfect."

Her belief was that they loved each other enough to weather any storm should storms arise and her commitment and determination were never in question.

It was true and Joseph didn't deny the fact that he had missed out on what some would claim should be considered as imperative training by role models in the family setting in which he was raised. But he insisted he'd had a great mother, which he had, and a close relationship with his maternal grandfather until several years ago when he had passed away. This had been his family and he claimed total personal immunity to any happenings in his forebear's lives and felt emphatically that any choices his father or paternal grandfather had made were pretty much irrelevant to his life.

"Everyone rows their own boat in life," was a statement Joseph would often make. He had a penchant for numerous little one-liner comments and expressed many of these with what appeared to be a degree of arrogance disclaiming any influence of generational or environmental factors in how a person's life is shaped.

It's been said that, *"a person does not know, what they do not know."*

Joseph's confidence displayed a total lack of any awareness of the reality of a "spiritual inheritance" since his understanding of inheritance was relegated to the most simplistic, literal sense. He understood inheritance to be either a material estate left by a deceased person or the fact that offspring will often carry obvious physical likenesses and similarities genetically to their parents and forbears.

The thought that there might be a *spiritual* inheritance or legacy was deliberately glossed over by Joseph. This was the point that Sarah argued should not be overlooked, for as she stood back as an objective outsider, she felt she could detect by what she had learned of Joseph's family background that a cause and effect influence was somehow in motion. She carried a sense that this shadow could in all likelihood, be cast over her husband and ultimately over her. Intuitively Sarah saw that people inevitably take on certain spiritual and soulish attributes of parents and forebears; every bit as much as those features which are physically inherited. She forthrightly declared that spiritual inheritance had to be real although no one else cared much for her speculations.

What Sarah sensed had validity, but not knowing how one should deal with such issues anyway, she found her concerns were balmed somewhat by her father's glib comment when she conferred with him and he bluntly stated that, *"everyone marries someone who is imperfect in some respect."* With these words echoing in her mind, she resolved in her own heart that Joseph would then be perfect enough for her.

Plans were completed and soon the wedding day came.

It was a grand wedding with little constraint, if any, on spending money. Sarah's father had business people to impress as well as family, so a lavish affair it became, in spite of Sarah's protestations that the event was collecting a list of guests she personally had no connection with whatsoever.

The Cathedral in the center of Christchurch was filled with guests and spectators alike as a beautiful crisp, early spring day dawned for the marriage of Joseph and Sarah. The Cathedral had been beautifully presented with magnificent floral arrangements. The damage that had occurred to the spire as the result of an earlier earthquake had long since been repaired and now the joyful bells rang in chorus for the city to hear.

As a bride, Sarah looked positively regal arriving with her father in an open coach with a veil and long train that extended almost a quarter of the way down the aisle of the church. The pipe organ thundered out a majestic rendition of the grand hymns selected as part of the wedding service. The bride's father had proudly given his daughter to become the wife of Joseph Pollock. The couple stood almost breathless with nervous excitement at the grandeur of the occasion as they said their vows and exchanged rings to symbolize and seal those vows.

Joseph had caught his mother's eye at the front of the congregation and flicked a quick, coy little smile her way but he had not yet caught sight of his father. He had been ambivalent at first about inviting his father. Having learnt that a positive response from Grayson had been received by the people making wedding arrangements on behalf of his future parents in law, Joseph had actually warmed to the fact his father would be attending. He naturally felt apprehension at the prospect of his parents being in relatively close proximity to one another after such a long separation. Just how that might work out, was a concern as he knew it was fraught with difficulty for both his mother and his father, not to mention his own mix of bewildering emotions.

At the conclusion of the wedding service the bridal party made their way to the church entrance where guests filed out, pausing to offer their best wishes and congratulations to the newlyweds. Joseph waited expectantly for his father. As the guests were almost out of the Cathedral, he began looking around anxiously. Where was he? Had he exited the church by some other way?

He had said he would be there but had he changed his mind?

Finally the last of the guests had exited and there was no sign of Grayson...anywhere. A special coach had been dispatched as an honor, to bring Grayson to the wedding and it would return him home later that evening.

But it became apparent there was no indication Grayson or the coach had arrived that morning at Christchurch Cathedral.

He felt a burning hot indignation rising within, which in itself made him angry. Why should he care anyway he reasoned...isn't it just what he should have expected? Joseph's somewhat usual darkish countenance brooded more heavily than ever.

"Don't be upset and let this spoil your day," said Emily who had glided in to slip her arm under her son's, fully sensing and understanding what he was going through.

"It's alright darling," Sarah quietly whispered, the smile on her face not abating for a second. "I'm sure something must have happened because I know he would have certainly wanted to be here today," she confidently asserted.

The wedding reception had been planned for in a country lodge surrounded by beautiful gardens all in early bloom with the onset of spring. Prior to the wedding breakfast, guests had been asked to gather in a large, very attractive park-like garden area where they would enjoy champagne and a delicious selection of tasty finger foods while the strains of a very fine stringed quartet played in the background. Meanwhile the bridal party was to be photographed in another part of the grounds.

It was just as the photographic session had ended and the bridal party was wending their way through the gardens to join guests, that a smartly dressed attendant brought a silver tray to Joseph with a folded piece of paper on it.

Reaching out to take the note, Joseph imagined it would in all probability be some pathetic excuse his father had concocted to avoid attending this special day. A feeling of bitter resentment and disappointment had begun to simmer since they had left the Cathedral. It dominated his thinking and was robbing him of the joy this very special occasion should have afforded. And Sarah sensed it.

"Let it go now...*please*...we did our part," she had urged.

"We should never have even asked him to come!" Joseph had replied through clenched teeth.

"What was the point any way since he declared long ago his level of interest..." his voice trailed off revealing the disappointment he really felt at what he felt was the latest of just more rejection.

Reaching out he took the folded note off the extended silver platter.

Unfolding it, he read the scrawled hand-written cursive writing:

For the attention of Mr. Joseph Pollock.

It brings me great sorrow indeed to have to inform you in this manner and on this occasion that I was called by a coach driver to the home of your father Grayson Pollock at 10.15am today.

Your father was dressed smartly apparently intending to attend your wedding but was found collapsed and in an unconscious state in the doorway. As his doctor I had been treating him for a complicated form of tuberculosis for the past year. I regret to inform you that I was unable to offer suitable help and that your father passed away shortly after my arrival.

I am truly sorry that this unfortunate news should need to be brought to you on this, your wedding day.

Yours truly
Dr. R. A. Murdoch MD

This was distressing news to receive under any circumstance but how would Joseph receive this on his wedding day? Quickly joining him at his side, Sarah had read the note and now asked for someone to find Emily as quickly as possible and bring her to them.

Within minutes the mother stood searching Joseph's face for what was wrong. Without saying anything he handed Emily the note. She read the note through then dropped it, staring ahead vacantly while it fluttered to the ground. It was only a moment before mother and son melted into each other's arms to hold each other in a silent embrace. There was a closeness here that had been fortified by the years of absence of a husband and father. Sarah could understand the bond and felt no level of threat or concern. Wisely she let her handsome groom and his mother take this moment to silently console each other.

There was grief of course but it was perhaps less intense than what might be anticipated had this family unit been intact rather than having become so fragmented over the years. Ironically for Joseph, it brought considerable comfort and relief to discover that his father had been fully planning to attend the wedding. It meant a lot. Somehow it helped soothe the angry bitterness he had felt when he had assumed his father must have simply contrived some reason or an excuse for not being there.

The news of course caused some degree of clouding over the day's proceedings but in most respects, the celebration of this young couple being joined as husband and wife, held precedence over any other consideration. The guests were informed of the death and a supportive sense of empathy accompanied the news as it inevitably began to ripple through the discussion and small talk of those present.

The bride's family proved to be wonderful, generous hosts and the lavish preparations made guests feel treated and highly honored. This was a wedding that had been planned with all the detailed refinement and accoutrement of the Victorian era. A fine three-course, sit-down banquet with expensive wines was brought to guests at their tables, each set and adorned with exquisite serving placements. The usual obligatory speeches followed.

Early evening saw the string quartet launch into a traditional waltz. The dancing began, led first by the newly weds and then others were invited to join the couple on the dance floor. It truly was an elegant affair. Joseph and Sarah looked very happy and while of course some thoughts of Grayson were underlying, the subject was not allowed to assume any prominence. Any planning and thinking about a funeral would have to wait.

And so it was Joseph and Sarah became Mr. and Mrs. Pollock. They began life together living in accommodations inside the city area that were owned by Sarah's father. Postponing their honeymoon arrangements briefly, they attended the small gathering at Grayson's funeral before following through with their plans. Granted it was a strained time for a young couple already embarking on the inherent adjustments of married life.

The funeral was a simple ceremony with Grayson being buried appropriately enough in the same plot as Thomas Sutcliffe—in fact their graves were within thirty feet of each other. Joseph was now grateful for the insistence of Sarah's encouragement to make the contact with his father given the circumstances that had subsequently unfolded. Knowing that an attempt had been made to extend *an olive branch* to his father, was certainly an easier scenario to manage than if Grayson had died in oblivion with no family contact.

There was still mystery around Grayson's life and his choices. The mistakes he had made and the many unanswered puzzles of the man had to be looked at within a certain context. Considering his past, his pains and the grievous circumstances under which he was wrenched out of all that was familiar to him as a nine-year-old boy living in London in 1850, it ought not to have been so surprising that he had grown up with such incapacitating wounds.

Deep inner wounds that are of a spiritual nature are not necessarily healed with the passage of time, unlike those inflicted on a person's physical body. The force of wounds on a person's emotional and spiritual life, becomes a legacy that is passed down to the next generation to live out of unless someone in the family line finally stands up having recognized what is happening, and breaks off the pattern.

Now the baton had passed to Joseph. What he would make of his life, would be shaped and determined to some degree by what he would do with the legacy he had inherited from his father...whether he recognized that as a fact or not. Joseph's confident assertion that, *"Everyone rows their own boat in life"* had some truth to it but it failed to take into account that there were significant, generational factors and influences in his family background that he chose to remain oblivious to.

15

ISSUES RE-VISITED

It was 1900, the year Canterbury celebrated its fiftieth year Jubilee.

Being the main center in the region, Christchurch was buzzing with a range of cultural and festive happenings as the nation celebrated entering the twentieth century! As a successful young accountant, Joseph had been offered and taken a partnership in his firm by now and was advancing in his career. It was a time of opportunity and Joseph was not about to waste a moment.

A lot had happened in the previous decade to move this successful colonial settlement into a thriving city center, at the hub of what was at the time, New Zealand's most progressive province. The technology for refrigerated meat exports was bringing prosperity to the area, Ballantyne's had become the first store to be lit by electricity, steam trams ran from Cathedral Square to the Railway Station and many civic works such as the development of roads and the creation of harbor boards had been undertaken by the development of Borough Council.

Having been married now for a little over four years, Joseph and Sarah had moved into a beautiful suburban home and were the proud parents of three year old James Hayden Pollock—a healthy and adventurous little boy who kept his mother continually busy while her husband struggled to juggle work and family responsibilities. At least he did try in measure to fulfill family responsibility initially by giving time to be with his wife and little boy. However there was always the sense of them having his "divided" attention.

For Joseph, the promise of reward for hard work and strategically positioning himself in the business community began to occupy not just a predominant part of his thinking but also the best part of his time and energy. He was ambitious, hard working and driven to achieve his goals. Each day he would set out for the office looking very sharp in dark suit, shirt and tie with business satchel in hand. Once gone from the home in the morning he would not return until dark each day of the working week as well as spending many hours during weekends on work related matters.

The priorities a person establishes in life are displayed by their practices and it would have to be said that Joseph had begun to demonstrate a tendency to make choices that may have been justifiable for business and financial reasons, but were detrimental and potentially dangerous for his family. Long hours took him away from family and he became pre-occupied with business-life and clients. This had the effect of gradually eroding Joseph's ability to give his best to his wife and son. He stoutly would resist any such charge and would defend his lifestyle saying "it was for the family" and declaring it was just for a season anyway.

But it seemed that the season was just never ever over…

It was not as if Joseph exactly had a corner on such behavior as it has always been a potential danger for husbands and fathers to operate in this manner thus unwittingly failing in their first and foremost priority.

Sarah tolerated the pattern to some degree having seen it in a measure with her own father. However her tolerance changed dramatically during a visit from Emily who came to stay. It was Christmas 1902 and this stay became a good deal longer than the one or two week visits that occurred occasionally. For Sarah, that visit became a turning point and she effectively established a point of demarcation. She was tired of little James getting the dregs of his father's time and energy and she wanted her husband back.

Emily was ageing but she saw in her son Joseph, that some disturbing patterns had developed. She astutely recognized what her son was doing. This grandmother observed what her son and five year old grandson James were like together as well as how her son related to his wife. Joseph's manner disturbed Emily greatly and she could not remain silent. Speaking cautiously at first to Sarah about these things, she described the particularly unhealthy propensity in the Pollock men to fail in their marriages and in their role as fathers. Together, in this context as they replayed and discussed the lives of Grayson and his father, as well as his grandfather, Sarah became greatly alarmed as it confirmed for her what she had known was happening. She had seen the desperate need for changes in order to apprehend the situation as far as Joseph was concerned.

She readily agreed at Emily's suggestion that Joseph and her should have a mother and son talk before she returned home. Emily placed great stock in what she believed was a strong bond of closeness between her and her son Joseph. She felt confident enough in the relationship with her son to believe he would be open to her heartfelt plea.

One evening Joseph returned home late and Emily rose from her bed and donned her night gown to take her son aside after wrestling with the issue deeply in her own mind. This mother had no desire to interfere but was wise enough to have identified something sinister that would ruin this family's life if left unchecked. She felt certain that the depth of mutual love and care in their relationship ensured that she would receive a responsive hearing from her son and that her well-intentioned talk would achieve a good result.

As quietly as she could, Emily slipped downstairs and approached Joseph as he sorted papers on the dining room table. She was very determined to secure the opportunity right then to sit with her son and to have a talk. She was burdened with the sense of losing her boy.

"Son, we need to have a talk please," she said gently.

"Mother!" Joseph exclaimed in surprise, "What is on your mind at this time of night? Surely…whatever it is can wait can't it?"

"This is important Joseph and *no*, it cannot wait any longer."

Her tone of voice and somber expression arrested Joseph and he pulled out a chair at the table where she joined him. She clasped his hands in hers and began…

"I want you to please listen to me carefully and to understand everything I have to say is motivated by my deep love and my concern for you," said Emily as she began her carefully thought out appeal.

She began to describe the ways in which Joseph's father had struggled as a husband and a dad. She recounted things Grayson had found he could not rise to, without going as far as to tear the man down. She talked about his father's obsessive ways and related how that having had the chance to observe her son's lifestyle, she was distressed enough to sense the need to mention what she perceived to be similarities. The driven-ness she described in Joseph could potentially destroy him and his family if left unchecked, she passionately admonished with tears in her eyes.

While she saw differing elements had bought about the destruction in the Pollock men and their families, she clearly identified the same pattern, even if the *means* of disintegration happened to vary.

Joseph listened, but gave no indication he had heard. Inside, he saw himself as being different from his forebears and felt his mother was being extreme and exaggerating the issue. He believed he was sufficiently "aware" to prevent any problem from ever arising, in spite of it being brought to his attention that a problem had arisen *already* and currently existed, that he was seemingly utterly unaware of.

He was courteous enough to listen to Emily while maintaining a patronizing and almost condescending aloofness. He thanked her for her concern but stated that she had no reason to be perturbed. He then wished her goodnight and stood up to pull the chair out from the table and let her return upstairs. Emily's effort to be an advocate for Sarah and the marriage seemed to have failed.

Long after Emily had gone home, Sarah's pleas for Joseph to modify his allocation of time and invest in his family more, increasingly fell on deaf ears. Her feeling of not being heard led her on two occasions in the following year to take James and travel to the farming homestead where Emily's family was. With the sheep station now being run by Emily's brothers and their sons, she lived a peaceful country life-style that contrasted starkly with the life-style Joseph sought to compel Sarah to live. Emily was glad at one level to see Sarah arrive with grandson James and felt obliged to offer a haven of respite for her daughter in law, but grew more troubled as she learned more of her son's increasingly busy life-style.

James was a particularly endearing little boy with a special capacity for affection and the company of his father, but tragically, here was a father who was allowing himself to become fully absorbed and pre-occupied with business and career. As time progressed there was no abatement in the pattern of Joseph's allocation of time. If anything, it grew worse as Joseph read Sarah's responses as being ungrateful in the light of the "life of privilege" he felt he had afforded her with his skills and efforts.

"You could not want for anything," he railed on her at times at times, "but it's never enough for you!"

"You don't understand, I do not want a life of privilege, possessions or status," Sarah would plead.

"It's our family that means more than things or position to me. You are a becoming a different person to the man I thought I married and I want him back," she would sob.

"Can you not see how much your son is reaching out for you Joseph?"

With the passing of time, distance increased. Sarah's father was a clear advocate for Joseph and he encouraged his daughter to do the "right thing" whatever that meant, in spite of the personal misery her married life had become. Feeling unloved, uncherished and superfluous to her husband's life, she began to look for a way out.

She could not change Joseph she reasoned but she could change her circumstances.

The old property owned by Grayson had passed in terms of his will, to Joseph and Emily. Situated in an area where new development was scheduled and property prices were set to rise, Joseph had persuaded his mother to adopt an approach of not making any decision quickly about what to do with Grayson's old home—rather to *"wait and see where property prices go"* before resolving in any way what to do with it.

It was to this aged, neglected looking property that with Emily's reluctant consent, Sarah took seven-year-old James to live for the next two years. Joseph saw his wife moving out as a treacherous betrayal and believed she was settling below her station as his wife. He was in all probability humiliated by Sarah's assertion of personal boundaries around her life. He still sought to pursue his own goals and made no effort to change his life or to hear her grievances. Instead, as ludicrous as it might seem, he seized the opportunity to accept what he saw as a prestigious opening. A lucrative and important career advancement had been presented, involving a move to another center in Auckland—the major city in the North Island of New Zealand. Unless they were to fall in with his ambitions, this meant a separation of many hundreds of miles from his family in Christchurch, the major South Island city.

For Sarah such an autocratic decision could in itself have been enough to spell the end of her marriage. By making such a move without any conferral with his wife, Joseph had thought it would force his wife to comply with his ideals. He believed a dutiful wife's place was to follow her husband come what may. While the decision her husband made to move was not the coup de grace for Sarah, what soon followed was. Joseph summarily put their fashionable home on the market and a sale was quickly forthcoming. It was a manipulative attempt to leave Sarah and James no option but to accompany him to Auckland.

The strategy failed as she chose to stay with James in the unkempt Christchurch home Grayson had owned. Sarah made the house clean and tidy but had little in the way of resources to renovate any part of the home—besides, it was located where properties were scheduled for redevelopment in the future, rendering it pointless to upgrade it to any major extent.

It was a strange thing to see the way James developed an affinity for this home of his grandfather's where he now found himself living, for all intents and purposes, fatherless, with his mother. It was a very sad state of affairs and one that might have been considered to be a highly likely outcome by anyone who had been appraised of the Pollock record of husbands and fathers. The situation had disintegrated into a state that was precisely what Emily had sought to warn her son Joseph of, but he had not heeded her warnings. Was all this mere circumstance? Coincidence? Bad luck or fate? Mis-management of personal life? Or was there more to it?

Sarah was a strong lady who was resilient in the face of her circumstances but loneliness and anxiety about her future were realities. There were times she berated herself for not being more diligent with the apprehensions she had felt about traits Joseph had exhibited before they were married. It was futile to reflect in this manner now but she found herself doing it all too often. She set about being the best mother she could be for James which helped stave off the projections of failure her own family put on her. The cute, mildly mannered little fair haired boy seemed to enjoy the scruffy old house they lived in with the overgrown garden and in particular the little upstairs attic. It was a place he often resorted to and would sit amongst the cast-off clothes Grayson had left up there along with piles of dusty old books, broken furniture, suitcases and dis-used household items. James had an active imagination and it was a fertile spot in the attic for dreaming up all sorts of adventures.

Little did he know how very significant this dusty neglected room would be in time to come, as far as determining his future was concerned.

James asked frequently about why his daddy was too busy to live with him and sought reassurance from his mother that his father cared about them. Something Sarah was uncertain she could offer any real assurance of, as her husband showed little evidence of being capable of caring about anything other than his work and the accumulation of money and status. It ought to be said that Joseph was not totally irresponsible as he periodically sent sums of money to his Christchurch office to be placed at Sarah's disposal for her and James…something Sarah accepted but cynically felt it was an act her husband undertook to placate his conscience.

Ironically Joseph, having severely judged his own father for the lack of "*thereness*" and contact during his childhood, had now begun to exhibit exactly the same behaviors he himself had resented. Sarah wanted James to grow up free from the legacy that seemed to be like a curse dogging the Pollock males and hoped to teach her son to be different. She feared he could precipitate the historical pattern and fretted about how to prepare him well for adulthood. The troubling thing to Sarah was how much of a stronghold this influence appeared to exert in propelling the men of this family into making foolish choices.

Having previously become acquainted with the circumstances of how Grayson's mother had seemingly concurred with the plan to ship her nine-year-old son off to New Zealand with Thomas Sutcliffe all those years ago, it had defied every motherly sense in Sarah. Now in the light of what she was experiencing it began to make a little more sense to Sarah and she sorrowed for that poor mother waving good-bye to her little boy from the window. Perhaps, she pondered, Grayson's mother had hoped the separation from his father by geographical change would also bring about change in the character of her boy's life and protect him as well from undesirable influences. It was a vain hope but in frantic desperation to achieve a purpose, people will revert to measures they may later have cause to regret.

The belief Sarah formed, was that Grayson's mother must have been a woman who never got over the *loss* of her son and the manner in which she "gave him up". She was resolute she could never let her James leave her side.

Joseph's departure was a deep source of grief to his mother Emily. It even impacted upon her health as for months as she fretted over the matter. Finally, Emily asked Sarah to leave the old home and come to the Barker family homestead where she and James could live.

Emily felt a high degree of empathy with Sarah and once she and James made the move, it would prove to remain a mutually comfortable arrangement for the next nine years.

Thus it was, the old property originally purchased by Grayson was left empty to languish, uninhabited, with Joseph many miles away, significantly removed geographically and emotionally detached from the circumstances of home and family.

16

VISITING THE OLD HOUSE

With the outbreak of war in Europe in 1914, the impact was felt not just in the theatres where battles were being fought and lives were being lost. In the colonies of Great Britain, young men from ordinary walks of life were sent to fight bravely and many families of New Zealanders would lose fathers, uncles, brother and sons in the defense of freedom.

James was only seventeen when World War One broke out and was too young to be called up for duty at that stage. It was a significant year in other ways for James as it was the year his grandmother died at the age of seventy-three. The passing of a matriarchal figure is a significant loss in any family and Emily was certainly that figure. Her funeral gathered an awkward composite of family members who had became estranged with the passage of time.

Joseph, still living in Auckland, made the trip south upon hearing his mother's health had slipped very low and that she was unlikely to recover. He had arrived two days after her death—well in time to attend her funeral but not in time to reconcile with her in any way. Now at her funeral he sat brooding in sullen silence throughout the service without mustering any voice at all to honor his mother and her role in his life. It was bizarre, inexplicable behavior from a son whose mother had done so very much and cared so deeply for him.

"Today we honor the life of a kind-hearted, wonderful woman who lived to give," Sarah bravely began her eulogy.

"My mother in law had a longing for family to be what it should be in spite of the disappointments she experienced herself and the sense of unfulfilled expectation she died still carrying in her heart..."

"Today a hole has been created in my heart that I will never be able to fill," echoed James.

"I'll always be thankful that my Gran was wise, gentle and was there willing to support in hard times..." his voice broke as he caught his father's eye, causing him to falter and lose any poise at all. Unable to regain composure, James seated himself again, his shoulders heaving as he placed his face in his hands and sobbed in pain. This was a soft-hearted young man who had grown physically and matured well in his grandmother's home under masculine guidance and direction from his uncles, Emily's brothers. Still fair-haired and now tall, he gave the impression he was older than his years.

In an emotionally charged setting, Sarah courageously managed the grief she felt at so many levels. She had of course lost a friend and confidante, not just a mother in law, and now the funeral had served to highlight the fact that she had also lost her husband and her marriage as well. James was there to farewell his grandmother but seeing his father reminded him that he had also effectively lost a father many years ago, the man who sat darkly in his own world during the service and who would scarcely acknowledge his wife and son once the service was over.

With the death of Emily, Sarah felt an era had closed and began to make plans to return to Christchurch in spite of Emily's family extending genuine, caring warmth and encouragement to stay on at the homestead.

James wanted to train in medicine but would have been required to complete some academic qualifications he had not met for entry to university. He was intelligent and eager to learn and motivated in applying himself to study.

Returning to Christchurch would allow him time and opportunity to pursue this path. A caring, gentle young man, his mother was proud of his growth and maturity given the struggles of essentially growing up fatherless.

James had a keen desire burning inside of him to find a life of wholeness and abundance, unshackled by the history of his predecessors. He was by now well appraised of the legacy of dysfunction that had characterized his family down through the generational line and it concerned him deeply. Was he merely a helpless pawn destined to emulate the traits of his forefathers? He thought not—at least he fervently hoped not. But how could he be free—unfettered, and how could he escape being the next victim to the relentless destructive forces that seemed to bear down on the Pollock family's relationships?

What might it take to break free and establish a more compelling generational line?

A measure of inclination towards "spirituality" was clearly evident in James and this, together with an enquiring mind had shaped his views and personality. *Spirituality* of itself was not something others of the Pollock men were devoid of—in fact to the contrary, but that quality had been seemingly swallowed and engulfed by other forces—and now it was James who carried that spark which held promise that a more noble destiny might be pursued and be fulfilled. Often in his mother's conversation, she echoed her hope that her boy's life heralded some possibility that the Pollock line might rise to a level of potential previously unrealized.

Sarah's family accepted James and her into the family home where comfortable self-contained living space was offered. There, this mother and her nearly adult son picked up their lives and purposed to move forward. The accommodation was private in a semi-attached apartment in the grounds of her father's home. Initially Sarah had concerns that being in close proximity to her father with the aspects of personality that characterized him, would be a problem. He could bring pressures and influences to bear that she would find undesirable. However such concerns never eventuated and it proved to be a comfortable arrangement. Within months of settling in, James was engaged in study and relishing the stimulation of a disciplined learning environment.

One day a legal letter arrived for Sarah. Joseph was relinquishing any claim on Grayson's old property which meant it was left entirely in Sarah's ownership since in Emily's estate, she had left her share to her daughter in law.

"I'd like to visit the old house one day mother," James announced randomly. At least it appeared random, whereas making a visit had been under consideration by him for months off and on.

"Why is it of interest to you James?" Sarah asked.

"That isn't something I even really know or have an answer for," he said truthfully.

"I know it's likely to be almost unfit for anything at all after this amount of time, but you wouldn't object to me paying a visit would you?"

"Well I can't be sure it's even safe after all this time."

The old home had indeed become more neglected than James or Sarah could have even imagined. Sarah believed it's real value lay in the appealing location of the land and believed that the building, although basically sound might have a limited future. She had little interest in it from a sentimental or any other point of view.

Somehow to James, it's value lay not in its commercial viability but in a certain inexplicable mystery it held for him. It wasn't sentimentality. Was it the excitement of childish games and imagination that he had found was sparked so vividly playing in the attic there years ago? Or did it hold other secrets waiting to be prised from its dusty timbers...?

The thought of visiting his grandfather's old run down house became a persistent thought until eventually James determined he would visit one particular Sunday afternoon.

"Mother," James began somewhat cautiously, "I would very much like to visit the old house tomorrow and wondered if it might be alright to have the key if you don't mind," he asked tentatively.

"Of course you may but can I ask you for what purpose you plan to visit the house?

"Well it's strange really…but I feel a strong connection with the place…almost a drawing there, even though it's been years since I was near the place…" his voice trailed off wistfully as memories of sitting in the old attic with its eclectic assortment of curious contents began to scroll across his memory.

James could even still smell the distinctive odors from the stacks of yellowing musty books and old clothes. The bits and pieces of old furniture scattered around and disused household effects, some of them damaged or broken had been fun for playing imaginative games with as a child. And there were of course the cobwebs. Cobwebs were everywhere then…what might it be like now he wondered?

"I have no idea what all these keys are for but here's what I have for the house," sighed Sarah as she placed a large bunch of assorted keys strung together on a piece of wire, some large and some quiet small, on the dresser.

"And neither James, do I have any idea what it is that is so fascinating for you about the house…but it doesn't bother me if you want to go there."

There were some very distinctive looking old keys amongst them and James picked them up looking quizzically at the collection wondering what purpose each may have had in its day. One interesting key had a little engraved disc attached to it with the letters *"TPS"* etched roughly into the dull metal surface. Another looked like it might be a front door key, one a back door key, another possibly for a padlock, while several looked like they may have been keys for suitcases or lockers… or something.

James felt almost a sense of thrill holding the keys. It wasn't the thought of all those ones from the past who had handled them or the history this bunch of keys represented, as much as, looking at them, they somehow seemed to represent future destiny to him.

It was a weird train of thought...that these keys actually in themselves were a *key to unlocking a future.* It was probably just the boyish love of adventure and imagination stirring but nonetheless James looked forward to going to the old property of his grandfather Grayson, with a great deal of anticipation. Almost a sense of being on a mission took hold of James while the reality was he had no idea what he was really going for.

Lost in thought, James quietly pedaled his bicycle along the way to the property while an odd battle started to originate in his mind as he got nearer to his destination. This was a little bit crazy really wasn't it? Why bother doing this anyway? There was no point to it surely...With only a mile or so to go James braked to a stop under a large oak tree. Pausing, he gazed up wondering about the age of the oak and the stories it could tell. He pulled the keys out of his shoulder bag and looked at them once again... for about the hundredth time since his mother had given them to him. That strange feeling still persisted that somehow these keys held a *'key'* for him and that they could unlock stories he needed to know. Discarding any thought of abandoning his mission he resisted that impulse and started off again with renewed vigor and purpose.

Arriving at the property, James was taken aback at how the house and grounds had slipped in condition in the years since he had been here last. That was his impression at least as far as he could remember anyway. But then he reasoned it had sat empty for years and it would be expected that it had become run being unoccupied for so long. Long straggly weeds had overtaken the lawns and creeping vines had invaded the trees around the house. The red painted iron roof was badly faded and the bare metal was yielding to rust. James wheeled his bicycle up through the scruffy knee high growth towards the steps at the front door. The paintwork on the house itself was shabby with moldy grime covering much of it. Some of the windows seemed to have been partially broken and it looked dark and foreboding inside. Startled, a pair of birds flew noisily from the pot on top of the old brick chimney that showed signs of disrepair with the mortar disintegrating.

There it was. James took off his cap, running his hand through his hair as he stood looking up at the attic window that was on the gabled end of the house above the little verandah. Treading carefully he made his way to the steps and up onto the verandah. Laying the bike against the weatherboards, James reached into his shoulder bag and pulled the bunch of keys out. Holding them, he selected the one he though most looked like it would suit the front door. It was a characterful old door with matching halves in moldings and panels with narrow windows that were rounded at the tops.

James inserted the key into the lock and turned it first one way, then the other. It was very tight and felt "gritty" but to his amazement the first key he'd taken a guess at, unlocked the door relatively easily and he turned the handle to open it. Pushing it forcefully the door creaked open on unused hinges, allowing a shaft of light to burst into the gloom.

James stepped inside…a little nervously. How long was it exactly since anyone had been in here he wondered to himself. Light caught the cobwebs that hung like chandeliers from the ceilings. The drapes were tatty and the wallpapering had given way in places cascading to the floor in large pieces. As James' eyes grew accustomed to the poor light he noticed there were still items of dust laden furniture dotted around the musty smelling lounge. He remembered Grayson's old armchair, now covered in dust, which had sat there unoccupied for so long. And there on the wall behind the armchair, was an old photo of Grayson's mother still gazing expressionlessly into space. His great grandmother had made an impression on him from the same spot when he had been there last as a nine-year-old boy. Sarah had explained who the *unhappy* lady in the photo was, in the best way a mother could explain to a young curious son who had a penchant for always asking questions. There were still the items on the mantle piece above the fireplace he remembered too…a candelabra, some book ends and a very strange vase. A rather nice little water-color painting of some climbing roses hung on the chimney wall. It was signed simply, *'Emily'.*

The fireplace was exactly how he remembered and walking around it through to the dining area, he found himself in the familiar dowdy kitchen. The old cream-colored enamel sink had ochre stains down it where a leaky dripping tap had once been at work. He swept his fingers over one of the bench-tops wiping a swathe of dust onto his trouser leg. James could smell a concoction of mice and ants mingled with accumulated damp, dust and mold.

The carpets were rotting and frosted around the edges with a white mold growing on them. It wasn't particularly offensive—it was just what one would expect in an old dis-used house. James walked through the hallway and looked into the bedrooms. There was still furniture in the places just as he remembered, including the little room where he had slept when his mother Sarah, first brought him as a lad to come to stay here. The lace curtains were falling to pieces and in most rooms there were pieces of patterned wallpaper hanging off the walls. Cobwebs hung off the light in his old room and he resisted an instinct to dust and clean things up. The wide bare timber tongue and grooved board floors in his room creaked as he trod over them. James wondered how his mother would respond to being here at this moment…

Making his way to the narrow stairway that led to the attic, James felt a mixture of trepidation and excitement. His heart pounded in his chest—something he was surprised at since it seemed a reaction disproportionate to the circumstance.

The stairs and wobbly balustrade rose steeply to a small landing, where the door into the attic was positioned. The door was shaped to hang on a rakish angle conforming to the pitch of the roof at that point in the house. James reached the landing and turned the little brass door handle. The door was locked. Of course, he thought to himself. One of the keys in the cluster, would almost certainly have to be for the attic door. He made his way back down the stairway without a clue what he'd done with the keys. Re-tracing his steps, he found them on the kitchen bench just where he had swept his fingers over the dust laden counter top.

Trying a couple of keys before selecting the correct one, James unlocked the door and had to push forcefully as it had dropped on its hinges over the years. The door graunched noisily over the surface of the wooden floor of the attic as it was opened.

Stooping slightly, James stepped inside.

17

ATTIC EXPERIENCE

It was remarkable. Like being in a time warp really.

The attic and its contents had remained unchanged even down to the placement of the items scattered around. And the smells too were the just the same as he remembered.

The books had a little more dust on them and perhaps there was a new generation of spiders laying claim to the area, but in most respects it seemed to be just as James had remembered as a nine-year-old.

Wandering around, it happened that he spied the large wooden sea chest that had belonged to Thomas Sutcliffe. Of course he'd seen it before during his attic adventures and knew that it had belonged to a very good friend of his grandfather. He had been curious what this large chest contained and as a boy he had been frustrated that it was locked and withheld its mystery.

Now at this moment, James stood there riveted, having just noticed that the carved letters on the chest, matched those letters which were etched on the disc that was with one of the keys in his possession!

Breathlessly he fumbled through the bunch of keys until he found the disc and the key with it. To his immense disappointment, the lock was unyielding as he tried the key. It was a very sloppy fit and while it could easily have seemed a mismatch, James believed the coincidence to have a key with letters that corresponded to those carved on the timber was just too great to discard. And so he persisted hoping it was just worn. Perhaps just getting the key in the right place would do the trick. Twisting and pushing the key into the lock and turning it in a variety of ways finally paid off! With a light 'clunk', James felt the lock tumblers eventually meshing with the cut of the key and simultaneously the lid popped up just a fraction…just enough to lift it. He slowly lifted the lid feeling a little intimidated by the loud protest of the creaking hinges.

James peered in.

Papers, bundles of letters and documents tidily gathered into piles and tied with string, some photos, surveyors plans, a compass with several other items that appeared to James to be navigational equipment, a number of woodworking tools were the things which first caught his attention as James carefully sifted through the laden chest. A little tin security box opened easily with one of the keys among the fistful in James' possession. In the little box was some worn English currency—notes and an assortment of coins. There were also handwritten receipts and payment dockets. It was all very fascinating. James knew vaguely of his grandfather's relationship with Thomas and had been told some of the stories concerning Grayson's arrival in New Zealand and the kindness Thomas Sutcliffe had shown to this young boy. James was aware of the circumstances of how Thomas had died in seeking to save Grayson's life. Some of the items in the chest had been put there by Grayson, including a very delicate, aged newspaper clipping which had been obviously folded and unfolded countless times. James read with a little difficulty the tatty article. It described the heroic gesture of Thomas Sutcliffe who had leapt to push Grayson Pollock clear of a bolting horse that was pulling a cart at breakneck speed through the street. His death had saved the life of the younger man and the article praised the bravery of Sutcliffe. It deeply moved James and he found within himself a strange sense of affinity with this man who had meant so much to his grandfather.

It was clear that deeply meaningful memories had resided among these keepsakes and trawling through the various belongings, felt for James, like he was being introduced to his 'roots' in a way.

There were books, notably a well-handled little Bible with Thomas' name on the flyleaf. It was marked with little comments in the margins and underlined throughout. James had never seen a Bible that had evidently been so well read and that meant so much to someone but it struck him as verging on sacrilegious to write in it and underline the pages of a holy book like the Bible.

It made a significant impression-but nothing like that which was about to impact him.

A large well-fingered, grimy envelope caught his attention.

Handwritten on the front, in very faded ink it said-

For Grayson James Pollock
PRIVATE & CONFIDENTIAL

James carefully lifted the flap to slide out a letter that also had the look of having been read and re-read countless times. Written by Thomas Sutcliffe, it struck James that what he was holding was an item that had obviously been very special to his Grandfather... evidenced by the amount of handling it had received.

Now, James began to read slowly...

My Dear Grayson,

I have wanted to talk a good deal many things through with you and feel I may have failed you in this. Forgive me for now broaching the subject in this manner but perhaps it will open some things for us to talk about. This seemed to me a way I could begin this conversation with you and it may of itself answer some of your questions.

There have been occasions when you have questioned me about your Grandfather, how it was that I was appointed to be your care-giver when the decision was made that you should accompany me to New Zealand. A decision that was made by your Grandfather in accordance with your mother's wishes. I do not believe your father was informed of the plans and I remain uncertain to this day, if he knows of your whereabouts...

Scarcely breathing, James read the letter with tears in his eyes. He quickly realized that the 'grandfather' being spoken of in the letter was the father of Grayson's mother—in other words, the *maternal* great grandfather of James. While he might not be acquainted with all the facts concerning his grandfather, Grayson James Pollock, or this great grandfather, the gaps in his understanding were rapidly filling in...and now this letter would give him some additional insights into the brokenness his grandfather experienced as a child. It was strangely captivating reading the letter and he marveled at how he felt somehow "connected" with the story.

In a way James felt like *he* was a continuation of *his* great grandfather's, *his* grandfather's and *his* father's stories. How his own father Joseph, could make the decisions he had made and the impact it had on him as a child had always been beyond comprehension. He acknowledged how hurt he had been with the absenteeism his father had displayed. How he had ached to be gathered up in his Dad's arms and to be assured of his love and to hear that he mattered to his father. What James was reading now offered some clues to a sinister propensity affecting Pollock father and son relationships that clearly ran in the family line. He could see how Grandpa Grayson had gotten *damaged* and how that hurt had in turn had become something his father Joseph had inherited. He could also detect the connection, even though it was likely to have been completely unintentional, that his father lived out, to pass on yet again. Even though the characters involved had made their own choices, it became clear to James that in a strange, mystical way his family line displayed a pre-disposition toward making choices that were so often destructive. Something was at work to produce this effect he reasoned.

James couldn't escape the feeling that he was personally implicated in an ongoing, unfolding story... In his mind were these ominous thoughts, *"It's my turn now...where will this stop...? What do I do with this...?"*

Thomas had continued his letter to Grayson...and James read on eagerly.

Much of what you have experienced, I believe I understand since in some ways it is not too dissimilar from my own story. As an eight year old I lost my family and your grandfather took me and gave me a home since there was no family member to care for me....

James was gaining a moving insight into some of his family legacy and it offered an account for much of the relational ruin down through the generational line of the Pollock family...The most stirring part was the last section in which Thomas Sutcliffe had left his worldly goods to Grayson, his grandfather...but it was more than that. It extended the challenge to secure a personal relationship with God and it was this that resonated so deeply with this nineteen-year-old young man. He felt on the brink of something...

It felt almost as if he was poised somehow to make a decision that could effect his life and determine the destiny of others coming after him.

I will be looking forward to talking with you once you have read this and become aware of these things. I hope that our conversation will be aided by this letter.

James had gathered enough from his reading, that this conversation which Thomas had planned to have with Grayson, would have never eventuated...

There is only one more matter and it is this. I have no living natural family. You are my closest 'family'. I am almost an 'uncle' but I feel in many ways you have become like a son to me and so, should anything ever happen to me Grayson, everything I own and all my material possessions will become yours.

The greatest possession that I have is something I cannot give you. That is my relationship with God through the Lord Jesus Christ and the gift of salvation. This is a matter I have spoken to you about many times. It is my prayer and desire that you will claim this treasure for yourself Grayson. With much love and kind affection.

Yours truly,
Thomas Pollock-Sutcliffe

James folded the letter and carefully slipped it back into the envelope. He couldn't help wondering if his grandfather had done anything about claiming the "treasure" that Thomas had urged him to. There was no way of really knowing with certainty, but given the outflow of the man's life it seemed most unlikely. Tears flowed freely down James' face. He hardly knew why, but it just felt right. Surely he was meant to be here in this attic, right now in this moment of time. It was like he was colliding with destiny and there was a sense of awe that began to catch hold of James. This *pull* or drawing he had been feeling to come here…it wasn't just a curiosity that was a hangover from his childhood. These items all around him were present back then but it was *now* that they were capturing him in a way that could have never happened when he was a child.

Fleetingly it crossed his mind that the desire that he had felt to come here was ordered by God. Had God wanted to meet with him *personally* and was He seeking to reveal things to James that would alter his destiny?

James had always been "hungry" for something that was missing deep inside. At times it resonated within him…the sense of futility and aloneness. It gnawed at him that if God was there, he had to find that reality and know that his life was not just a meaningless moment on the *stage of life*.

James placed the things he had removed back into the chest carefully and closed the lid. The afternoon was passing quicker than he had realized and the light was now starting to fade. Turning his watch on an angle to catch sufficient light from the only light source in the attic—the large window on the gable end of the house, he checked the time. Surprisingly he'd been there almost two hours.

A little dark, blackish colored leather suitcase caught his eye as James sat on the floor scanning the room and its contents. It was sitting perched on one of the piles of books as if it had been someone's intention to keep it up off the floor. He stared at it for a moment before deciding he had to check out its contents. Here was something he didn't recall ever noticing before. Strange it was, that he hadn't seen it because now it particularly had his full attention.

Oblivious to spider's webs and the dust on the floor that he was crawling through, James made his way over the ten feet or so, across to the books and lifted down the case. It was covered in a layer of dust. Pulling a neatly folded handkerchief from his pocket, James dusted the suitcase lightly with flicking movements and discovered just how old this weather-beaten little suitcase looked. It wasn't really black after all, but was a burnt umber, brownish color with large orange-cream colored stitching around the edges. Judging by its shabby condition, with bangs and bruises all over it and rather poorly repaired leather bound handle, there was no doubt, this little suitcase had some history and a good few stories to tell!

Discovering it too was locked, James again resorted to searching through the bunch of keys without too much expectation of finding an appropriate one to open the odd little case. There were only two reasonable choices in the assortment and surprisingly, once again, with the first attempt, the selected key slid into the small keyholes in each of the clasps on the lid and popped each of them up in turn.

The very instant that James raised the lid, truly the most remarkable thing happened simultaneously…!

With precision that could not be contrived, right at the very moment James lifted the lid, clouds outside parted, allowing a brilliant shaft of sunlight to burst in through the attic window. The formerly dull attic was flooded with light beams and surrounded James as if he was under some kind of divine spotlight! Completely taken aback, the young man gasped. But that was not all.

There was a sense of an awesome Presence that entered the attic room along with the beams of light. It was not a subjective figment of his imagination but James was experiencing a tangible, objective reality. It filled him with a sense of wonder and awe. The Presence was gentle but seemed to be firmly leading and compelling this young man to linger and discover more. Whatever *"more"* might happen to be. James was being drawn towards something warm and loving, something irresistible that was tender, not condemning, but offering forgiveness and healing.

He began to recognize that the sense of being drawn to this place in the first instance, had been *because* of the Presence. Now it was dawning on James that the whole idea of making this visit here hadn't even been his own idea after all. James felt like he was being invited to participate in something mysterious and that he needed to be given *light* in matters that he had only marginal understanding of.

Somehow James knew instinctively that the Presence was indeed God Himself—and He wasn't distant or brooding or punitive, rather He was coming as a loving Father…a Father who wasn't absent, neglectful or inadequate…the *father* the broken Pollock family line had so desperately needed for such a long a time. James was an eager and a humble student, only too willing to co-operate with this divine Presence.

What was it about this place and what was it about this little brown leather case? It seemed to be shrouded in light and he felt as if everything else other than the case became peripheral and inconsequential.

James' life would be changed forever beginning with the day he unlocked his grandfather Grayson's suitcase. Back in 1850 it had accompanied a totally lost and broken boy not quite ten years old in a sad, traumatic departure from England. Grayson through no fault that was his own had been sent away by a misguided family carrying his tragic, meager little collection of worldly goods. But more significantly he was carrying something else too, which could not be seen...an *"inheritance"* which was already ticking away and set to progressively unfold.

Carrying his little suitcase on board the ship about to leave Plymouth and set sail for New Zealand, he also carried *inwardly*, a deep feeling of confusion, rejection and shame that would shape the course of his entire life. This young child had been forcefully severed from all that was familiar and it created within him the feeling of not "belonging" and it had fractured his sense of personal identity. Grayson had felt those things acutely and the damage had never eased even as he grew older. The scars of being separated from a father and mother and family had gone deep, relegating this child to life with a wound on his spirit that the passage of time in itself, proffered little hope of ever eradicating. It would not have taken much of a prophet to foretell that this boy would carry a marred "legacy". The nature of this legacy would jeopardize his ability to formulate trusting relationships, and it would deliver a deficit in his personality that served to truncate the ability to nurture and cherish those who might ever be closest to him.

And so it was the child grew to manhood...a broken individual who lived as a captive within a prison without walls, destined to carry past pain and hurt that lay lurking below the surface into a marriage where his wife's loss of expectation and yearning to be cherished and nurtured could not be met...he would father a son but through lack of love and emotional nurturing would replicate the same dynamic as the fathers before him... having no clue how to in turn, be a good husband and Dad. In all likelihood over time, he was set-up as a ready candidate to be the conduit through which the same tempestuous emotional dynamic in *his* life, would inevitably be re-visited, even perpetuated in subsequent generations.

But the remarkable thing was now, that here in this moment so many years later, the lost, searching *grandson* of that boy, was encountering something of life-changing significance. He hadn't just found a key to unlock a suitcase…he was about to find a "key" which would unlock his life, allowing him to discover treasures that transcended anything this world could ever offer.

18

A DEFINING MOMENT

James sat there, surrounded in warm light looking through the contents of his grandfather's suitcase.

Being quite small, the case did not really contain a lot…a little pair of dried up, withered old leather shoes, some nondescript photographs, an oilskin coat with other items of clothing belonging to a small child, books, a couple of school exercise journals and a very beautifully crafted little compass in a black felt bag with a draw string on it. Funny how it was this gift from Thomas Sutcliffe which had delighted Grayson on his tenth birthday, that was an object that still held fascination for Grayson's nineteen-year-old grandson as he sat there examining it carefully all these years later.

But it was to an old leather bound hand-written journal, that James felt particularly drawn. Was it his imagination or did the light become brighter as James picked it up and examined it carefully?

For some reason it had string bound around it numerous times then it had been tied tightly in a series of clumsy knots. It had the appearance of having been in the hands of someone who had become frenzied in their intention of sealing it up. The distinct impression James formed was that someone had been unwilling to actually destroy or part with the item, but as a means of concealing its content had endeavored instead to keep any revelation the journal contained, inaccessible because it was all bound up. It was very strange. Struggling with undoing the bound up journal, James had intuitive insight that his grandfather Grayson had *never* become acquainted with what the writing inside was about…

With great difficulty James eventually removed the irritating string and began flicking slowly through the neat cursive writing. The name and written address on the fly-leaf, the dates and the contents themselves of the journal made it self evident that this was indeed the actual journal of Grayson's father…the great grandfather of James!

James quickly became absorbed in the passion that leapt from the pages. It seemed to be the attempt of a man filled with bitter remorse to purge himself of regret by writing out a confessional of his failures and his deepest inner feelings. Here was a man who was unburdening his soul. While acknowledging his mistakes and poor choices, it seemed apparent he had understood important truth but stopped short of exercising the faith to make a personal decision to receive grace that would bring forgiveness and freedom. The language was deeply thoughtful in a tormented kind of a way as well as being haunting at the same time.

James became captivated by a passage his eyes had fallen on…

"I am a mystery to myself, finding that I became at some point propelled to do things and be a person that I neither recognise, nor ever wished to be.

Having become caught up in an emotional nightmare I find myself now entangled in a web of deceit of my own making—having never meant to hurt anyone, I now fear for those poor souls whom I have hurt beyond imagination. I am a disappointment to myself, to others, and no doubt to God. The two women to whom I have been the cause of inestimable pain, little deserved the treatment I have dealt to them. Grayson my son I have also hurt...possibly destroyed?

I can hardly care anymore for myself but what might become of him? I hope you are able to forgive me as you read these pages son.

James read on…transfixed by the pages and absorbed by the raw emotion in the journal.

Of late I have turned to look again at the Holy Scriptures in desperation for some guidance. Is it too late for me as I suspect? I hope it is not too late for my little children.

In Proverbs of the thirteenth chapter and verse twenty-two, I have read something that has greatly troubled me that I know not what to do with.

To James it seemed like the handwritten verse that had been underlined, had been somehow earmarked for his personal attention. It arrested him as he read it several times, pondering the full meaning…

"A good man leaves an inheritance for his children's children."

What was to follow made things clearer still for James…

I am disturbed by the thought of what 'inheritance' I may leave for my descendants for I am not a good man and it seems logical to me that if a good man leaves a good inheritance so too an evil man will leave to his children's children an evil inheritance.

It troubles me greatly to contemplate what will become of Grayson and my descendants in the light of my choices and actions. Oh wretched man that I am! What is to be done? Can what is done be undone? In my present state I do not know, but this I do know...I have seen the longing in his eyes as he wanted me to reach out to him and find his heart but... I could not.

Is something dead inside of me? If so, can it live again? Can it live in him?

Did my own father fail me and now I must be sentenced in turn to failing my son? Will he too fail his son?

What inheritance can I leave him and what will he and his children become? Can I now be responsible with things for which I have been reckless and irresponsible?

James read the agonizing questions of this man with a lump in his throat as though feeling the anguish of his great grandfather expressed in pen and ink. Tears filled his eyes as he felt like a veil was being lifted off his understanding.

Of course…the connection was very clear…his father Joseph, was a product of his father's choices and now he himself was a product of the same inheritance. It was to become even clearer as he read on…

It has become apparent to me in the reading of Holy Writ that there may be some hope after all. Not that I can see how it lies within my ability to bring any change in this late stage of the journey.

Yesterday I read in the Book of Exodus 34 verse 7

"...keeping mercy for thousands, forgiving iniquity and transgression and sin and that will by no means clear the guilty; visiting the iniquity of the fathers upon the children and upon the children's children, unto the third and to the fourth generation."

The Lord God has made it plain that iniquity is bound to travel down a family throughout the generations even to the third and fourth. My first instinct was that the Lord was waiting with a vengeful spirit to visit wrath-filled judgment upon the hapless family coming after the guilty one.

Now I see it differently. The Lord has already announced Himself previously to be kind and gracious and full of compassion—so he cannot argue against Himself.

Yes, I am certain now, that what is being described is a principle that is set in motion and is irrevocable...a man is responsible for his evil acts of commission personally, but the problem is, the weight of these iniquities will force open a doorway into the seed of that man (his descendants), so that they being already pre-disposed and vulnerable are then by their OWN choices, as inheritors and partakers of his sins. Thus the father's iniquities are visited or passed upon the children...

Surely this was so with Adam for the scripture says, "in Adam <u>all</u> have sinned..." but... I see there is hope for it declares that a new lineage is possible in Christ. A new inheritance...

Perhaps the evil legacy I feel I am leaving for my offspring can be halted by one who will decide to follow Christ, to find forgiveness and release for our family from the curse I have introduced. My fear would be that until such a one in the Pollock line takes such charge, thereby disallowing the transfer of evil inheritance, it may well perpetuate further. God forbid that the harvest of iniquity should define the Pollock line. May it be that someone will stand up to reject bitterness and unforgiveness ...for by this only, may the old be eradicated and a new inheritance of righteousness be instigated.

Will there be someone to claim the promise of Romans 10, the thirteenth verse?

"Who ever calls upon the name of the Lord shall be saved."

Who will accept the legacy that awaits...?

The words seemed to almost burn as they penetrated deeply into James' soul.

It was as if the question had been specifically directed to him and it provoked a cry inside of this nineteen-year-old young man.

James' life stretched before him. But what might become of him, now pivoted on the decision he was about to make. Here he was, another *"fatherless"* young Pollock who could readily follow in the way of his father and of his father before him...and who could blame these ones when their stories were told, each of them for feeling the angry pain of bitterness and abandonment in their souls?

The legacy of fathers and husbands failing and falling from their task had resulted in generations of shallow, broken relationships and family disintegration. It was an indisputable, historical fact in the Pollock family line. And now James was being challenged with the thought of being the one to stand tall and reject the inheritance that had characterized his family for generations. He saw the stark reality. Either reject it and forgive his forebears or be destined to reap a similar harvest in his own life.

What would it be?

Would the future hold emptiness, broken relationships, loss and loneliness? Or would the offer of exchanging all that for a brand new legacy with a future of promise and hope prevail?

James now sensed that he was about to apprehend some kind of higher destiny that had beaten in his breast ever since he could remember.

The pain of having been rejected by a father who had failed, was being washed away with the warm sense of invitation he felt. He could release himself from unforgiveness and the 'old' could be exchanged for a new identity and purpose…there was a heavenly Father who was reaching out to wrap him in arms of love the way he had so wanted his earthly father to.

"I must have this *new* inheritance…!"

Falling headlong on his face with complete disregard for the grime and dust on the floor, James began to cry out aloud. Indifferent to all that was around him apart from the abiding sense of the Presence, James cupped his face in his hands and from the core of his being, began to pour out his heart. Tears streamed in rivulets down the dust caked face of this desperate young man who scarcely knew how to form the words…but the words were less important than the sentiment and depth of feeling behind them.

It was sufficient that he meant business in finding a personal friendship with God and that he was now relinquishing any sense of self-sufficiency and in humility reaching out for help. Having become acquainted with his need, James could now clearly see his own responsibility and what he needed to do to become free…

"Here I am God… I cry out to you. I ask you to save me and to turn me from willful rebellion. I do not wish to live my own life apart from you anymore. I want your *new* inheritance for my life…not my old self-led inheritance. Please forgive me as I choose to forgive those who have hurt me. I will not judge my father anymore and I'm sorry I have been so bitter and angry. I receive the new life that Jesus offers in exchange for the old and I reject every influence and undesirable inheritance of my natural family that would hold me back. Please let me be free and make me a new person today…"

The words flowed as James expressed his feelings to God, yet it did not seem as if using exactly the *right* words was that important.

It was the heart behind them that mattered…and somehow James just knew that God was being attentive.

This Presence, was just not an impersonal force but the heavenly "Father" who seemed to bore right into his inner being with beams of liquid love and acceptance. He knew that he had been *heard* and he knew that he was welcomed. He wept freely with tears of release and joy. It felt like chains that were binding him on the inside were being broken and that a great weight was being lifted off him somehow.

A deep sense of peace settled upon James as he arose from his face-down position on the dusty timber floor. He knelt for several minutes as the Presence seemed to be rejoicing and almost *dancing* around him. It was amazing… as if the light filled the entire room for a moment…and there was such peace.

James even *felt* lighter as he stood and stretched. A sense of joy filled him as he drew himself to his full height extending uplifted arms above his head.

He was different. It felt as if those chains that had bound him and that he was not even fully aware of before, had now fallen to the ground and he had stepped out of cold, unrelenting manacles into freedom. He felt loved by God and overwhelmed with the realization that his Heavenly Father delighted in him…it was like coming "home."

Oh how for such a long time, he had ached with a grievous pain for his earthly Dad, Joseph, to show delight in him…but now that was all washed away. Thoughts of seeing his Dad were no longer dread-filled…any thought of protecting himself from further hurt by his father's distant aloofness had gone. He anticipated seeing him and hugging him with genuine warmth and affection. Such a thought was radical considering the awkward walls that had been constructed and that had existed between this father and son.

James now realized that dusk had fallen and he was somewhat startled to notice how dark it had become outside. The space in the attic had seemed to be so full of light and he had lost track of all time. His mother could be concerned for his whereabouts.

Closing the door to the attic behind him, James walked carefully down the darkened stairway into the lounge area being careful not to walk into any of the objects scattered around in the gloom. He made his way to the front door and stepped out into the cool evening air. Breathing in deeply, James felt an indescribable sense of peace and wellbeing that he had never known before. He locked the old wooden door behind him and walked to the bicycle knowing he was leaving as a different person to the one who had first arrived a few hours previously.

It was strange but the "Presence" he sensed was with him in the attic hadn't merely remained up there once he had left and locked the door behind him. Cycling through the darkened streets towards home, James experienced a joy he had no words for. He would never be alone again. Words of gratitude fell from his lips as he talked to God as Someone who was with him…closer than breathing.

It dawned on James that this must surely have been something like what Thomas Sutcliffe had been describing in the writings he had left in the big wooden chest. Of course!

Now James wanted a Bible too…just like Thomas had. Maybe he'd ask his mother if the heavily marked Bible back in the old chest might be something he could look after for a while. After all, it seemed to James as if he might be the first Pollock in a while, at least as far as he could tell, that had shown any inclination towards the realities he had become awakened to.

James felt free… he would *never* be the same again. There was another aspect to what had happened to James as well…one that he might not have fully appreciated at that point. The transformation in him, opened up the possibility that the Pollock family line to come would never be the same again either.

19

KEPT UNDER FIRE

She was a beautiful girl, exceptionally easy on the eye but with an attractiveness that went beyond mere physical appeal. There was a grace and a charm about Hannah that affected even the atmosphere around her. She carried a presence about her and when she entered a room people noticed. Uncouth men who might normally be inclined to resort to base language and behavior would check themselves in the company of this lady. Naturally unpretentious, Hannah's regal bearing was far from snobbish sophistication but a simple beauty emanating out of an inner radiance that appeared to almost cause her to glow.

Even dressed in her prim, rather dour nurses uniform as she made her way through the ward attending to those who had been inflicted with the worst injuries, Hannah was a breath of fresh air bringing hope to the poor soldiers she served.

Her compassion for these servicemen who had been wounded, particularly those who had been maimed and irreparably damaged, was clearly evident. She was not immune or aloof to the sufferings and pain these men endured but reached out in mercy to alleviate their distress utilizing the skills her training had equipped her with.

It was 1917 and for three years World War One had inflicted terrible miseries on humanity across Europe, the Middle East and Northern Africa.

Brockenhurst in Hampshire, England was important as the location of a major New Zealand Military Hospital, for here, many of the New Zealand soldiers who were injured in battles from places in France, across the Western Front and Gallipoli were attended to. Within the grounds of the hospital a cemetery already contained the graves of the growing number of wounded New Zealanders who had sadly, in spite of the dedication of medical professionals, succumbed to their injuries.

In the First World War, between the years of 1914-1918, New Zealand paid a huge toll in making its contribution as a member of the Allied forces with 100,000 men signing up to fight for King and Country. It was regarded as a remarkable and a courageous effort from a relatively fledgling nation with a total population of only one million people. During the years that the war raged, over 18,000 New Zealand soldiers lost their lives and over 40,000 were wounded in grievous battles. It marked a hitherto unprecedented scale of human casualties and changed forever the way wars would be fought.

It was against such a backdrop that Hannah, a young, English born and bred nurse had sought and found opportunity to put her training to use in the hospital at Brockenhurst, helping wounded New Zealand servicemen. The dedicated care of nurses such as Hannah made all the difference in lifting the spirits of the injured as for many of these victims of war a high morale could make the difference between pulling through to recovery or languishing. Often it was the nursing staff who were credited for maintaining the morale of men whose bodies had been broken and it was they who also ensured these soldiers were not broken in spirit as well.

A young man she was charged with attending to, had caught Hannah's attention in particular. He lacked the roughness of many of the soldiers and his demeanor marked him as being different from the majority of his contemporaries in the wards.

Hannah learned this young man had only just turned twenty-one and he was not a combat soldier. He was a medical orderly who had sustained injury himself while in the course of duty somewhere in Palestine.

This young man was James Pollock.

James had gone to war. Holding strong convictions that drove him to search and find a way to serve usefully other than in a full combat role, he had found an opening where the medical training he had been receiving to that point could be deployed in a very meaningful way.

At twenty years of age, James had been assigned as part of medical back-up to a regiment known as the Canterbury Mounted Rifles. The regiment consisted of approximately six hundred horses, the majority being *'riding horses'* with the balance being draught and pack-horses. The CMR had been first formed in 1914, and was sent initially to Egypt for training.

They had then been sent to Gallipoli in 1915, going back to Egypt for four months, before serving in the Sinai in 1916 and then on to serve in the Palestine Campaign of 1917.

It was at this juncture that James received his orders and became attached to the Canterbury Mounted Rifles regiment as a medic.

At full strength the CMR had 26 officers and 523 other ranks and consisted of a headquarters staff, a machine-gun section and three squadrons. Each squadron had a total strength of 158, divided between a headquarters and four troops. Each troop was made up of eight four-man sections. Sections were tight-knit units; each man had a defined role, both in battle and in camp. In mounted rifles units, *trooper* was a soldier's rank equivalent to *private* in the infantry. Mounted riflemen were expected to ride to the scene of a battle but would often dismount and go into action as normal infantrymen as well as engaging the enemy on horseback where it was required.

Carrying out patrols and reconnaissance over larger areas than could be covered on foot, was also one of the roles of the regiment. While assisting wounded troopers one night in open ground, James and another medic had come under a counter-attack and found themselves pinned down in crossfire. From the outset, being subjected to the ghastly sights of wounded and dying men had affected James deeply, but there was a strength and poise about this young man that anchored him—even in extremity. Observing that a fellow medic evidently lay lifeless on the ground beside an injured trooper, James had bravely struggled to drag first one and then another two wounded soldiers to a place of cover. In the process James himself sustained serious injuries from shrapnel.

James was transported to Port de Korbeh Hospital in Egypt for surgery and an expected period of convalescence.

During the time he was recovering there, operational changes meant that most of the staff of this hospital were transferred to Brockenhurst and several patients including James were also sent on there as well for further recuperation. He had plenty of time for reflection and often pondered the seeming arbitrary nature of war, when one life might be taken and another preserved. Often the banter among soldiers was around who was *lucky* and who was *unlucky.* James quietly concluded that whereas others had perished, it must be for some reason he had been kept safe even under fire, by the intervention of "higher hands".

Ever since his "attic room" experience, James had lived his life consistently with a sense of purpose and destiny that he attributed to God at work in his life. Now lying uncomfortably in a hard, narrow hospital bed in England, far from home, wrapped in bandages he contemplated the path that his life had taken. What a remarkable sequence of events had unfolded that he should be in this place. In reality it was a miracle he was alive at all, given the scope of the skirmish that had claimed the lives of a number of his colleagues and inflicted injuries upon him that, while they had initially presented as life-threatening, he would survive.

He was grateful to have not bled to death and saw his preservation as the result of some kind of *divine* interception. Initially his thoughts would turn repetitively to troublesome questions and to wondering *"why"?* What might be the purpose for his life from this point on?

Whereas many found their lives stalled or derailed by the horrors of witnessing war, the things he had seen and experienced left their mark in terms of a heightened desire to make something purposeful of his existence. In all these musings James felt a growing calm and a peace that having come thus far, a positive future was assured. He felt a rest coming into his soul that he knew was God's work; something that sadly so many in his hospital ward knew nothing of. Frequently at night there would often be heard in the darkness, men moaning or crying out in agony of mind and body, and chilling screams from tormented souls as they re-lived some horrendous circumstance they had experienced on the battlefield. The nights were often worst and most patients looked forward to the light of day.

James grew to look forward with increasing eagerness to the professional attentions of the pretty young English nurse Hannah. In the light of this being a pressured under-staffed military hospital, she was part of a team that kept a busy and stressful schedule nursing the wounded and obeying the orders of the handful of doctors. The medical staff worked under extremely difficult conditions and daily, the numbers of wounded were added to. Working with inadequate resources as well as battling relentless tiredness, this young nurse seemed to have a certain grace about her that was noticed by all.

James had no wish to commandeer Hannah in the light of all the needs of the others lining the narrow ward, but it occurred to him that it was she who took time and extra care when it was his turn in the routine of being attended to. Hannah found it easy to converse with James, recognizing something different in this young man. She felt drawn to the depth of character and maturity that she saw unfolding as she gradually discovered pieces of his story and his background.

Hannah had listened with wide eyes as James opened up to her and recounted his experience in his grandfather's attic with God. As it turned out she too had a deep personal faith in God as the result of an encounter that had changed her life as a young girl. James had not been surprised to learn of her faith and felt certain that it was this dimension to Hannah that made her as beautiful as she was.

Six weeks after being admitted to Brockenhurst, James was discharged and remained in a hostel for a month during which time he received papers to say he would be rejoining the Canterbury Mounted Rifles. The news was surprising to James but to Hannah it was nothing short of devastating. They had found opportunity for time together after James had been discharged from hospital and she had continued to grow in her feelings for this gentle and sensitive young New Zealander. They had talked about so much including learning of one another's backgrounds that as it happened, proved to contrast quite dramatically. Hannah was a year or so older than James and had grown up in a rather privileged family that could track a proud lineage back for nearly two whole centuries. There had been a solid stability in her family no doubt in part, attributable to a faith in God that had been outworked and demonstrated with works of charity and social concern.

James of course had no such illustrious legacy to share but told frankly his family history as he knew it. Making no attempt to gild the lily, he had described the story of his grandfather Grayson's departure from England and all that had unfolded.

James described how his experience with God had changed him and left him with a clear revelation on how families passed on an inheritance that transcended that which was temporal, from one generation to the next. His emotions were very tender and his voice broke at intervals as he softly recounted the story. It wasn't that he was weak—far from it. People did not come through the situations James had been through without considerable personal courage and fortitude. Hannah listened appreciating the candor with which he spoke and as she did she sensed that here was a man she could trust.

Now with James receiving orders to rejoin his regiment they were being forced into facing saying a good-bye which they both dreaded.

It would be very hard as it was clear to both James and Hannah that a mutual *fondness* had grown between them. Actually if they were to admit it in their hearts, for both of them it was more than just a mere fondness. War did a strange thing for many couples who were brought together in circumstances that presented little or no future certainty.

It was natural to steel oneself against loss and heartache in such changeable, unpredictable times and adopting a certain casual exterior was common. Yet James had fallen in love and now believed that perhaps the reason that he had even been sent to Brockenhurst had been divinely ordained and felt that perhaps the reason was to meet this beautiful young lady. He suggested to Hannah that the fact their paths had crossed was ordered by guiding providence. She had looked deeply into his eyes as he explained the conclusions he was coming to while listening intently, nodding slowly…wordlessly, in agreement.

During the week just before James was to rejoin the regiment, he took a two-hour journey by train with Hannah to meet her parents one afternoon for the first time in their family home. They were charming folk who readily warmed to James over tea and scones. He could not help but make a mental comparison between this family with its rich heritage of faith and endeavor, with the dynamic of his own family.

Inwardly James had accepted a mandate that starting with him, the future of the Pollock family would be different. This had been his prayer on a regular basis. Later that day as they travelled by train back to Hampshire, he told Hannah he wanted *her* to be a part of a new future with him. It wasn't a direct proposal but it was direct enough to confirm for Hannah that this young man was serious in his intentions.

Their talk during the return journey centered around what the future might look like when the war concluded and they made promises and commitments to one another that they would write regularly, not allowing distance to cause permanent separation.

Parting would be difficult for both of them but it did help to balm the situation knowing that there was a general sense that the War was winding down. Their hope was that some day soon life might resume with a semblance of normality once again. It was an emotional day when James and Hannah had bowed their heads and with hands held, prayed together just a few short hours before James was due to depart. Their prayer was that God, who had seen fit to bring their lives together in England would protect them and that the same guiding providence that had brought them together in the first instance, would ensure that they were re-united safely in due course.

With that, he was gone. Five weeks later James was back with the Canterbury Mounted Rifles in Palestine.

After the armistice with the Ottoman Turks in 1918 the regiment was sent back to Gallipoli as part of an occupying force. The Canterbury Mounted Rifles later disbanded and most of its officers and men embarked on the troop ship *Ulimaroa* for the return voyage to New Zealand. Among them was James, heading for Christchurch where he would pick up his studies again and continue the regular routine of writing to his lovely Hannah. Settling back into post-war life was not easy for anyone. For James it required a lot of adjustment and it took some time before the feeling of displacement began to subside.

It did not help to ease the situation for James to receive no mail at all from Hannah for over two months. Naturally enough, this initially caused some anguish but James correctly surmised that the problem lay with a postal service fraught with difficulty rather than any indifference on Hannah's part. James felt securely anchored in the commitment they had made to each other and trusted that the promises they had exchanged before parting in England had substance. So it was he waited patiently to hear news from her. The occasion of first receiving a letter from Hannah was a euphoric moment for James! Once the letters started flowing from England they weren't to stop. James dreamed he was with Hannah and longed to be able to talk freely again without the vast distance that separated them.

This was a relationship that proved there is truth in the saying, *"Absence makes the heart grow fonder."* Every day, thoughts of

Hannah consumed James. His letter writing to her was prolific and he eagerly awaited her equally frequent replies. Hannah waited patiently for James to take some definite initiative to purposefully move their relationship forward. James was a creative planner and blessed with imaginative flair. A plan had been formulating in his mind and he had begun to carefully strategize its timing and outworking. It sustained him, filling him with hope as he eagerly anticipated the day that lay ahead, when they would be as one.

He dreamed he was with her and holding her close. How he longed for that moment when he would once again be able to talk freely face to face… without the vast distances that separated them.

EPILOGUE

Laughter and the sounds of celebration were in the air. The excited voices of children filled the house. A central focus of their attention was a silvery haired old man sitting in a large comfy chair he had just been presented with. It had a huge big golden ribbon trailing from it, which several of the children played with around his feet. He loved them and they knew it.

One little boy, the youngest, had crawled up and sat on his grandfather's lap, his eyes shining as he looked into the gentle, aged face of the one he adored. On the other side of the room this little boy's daddy looked on with pride and gratitude swelling within him. Scanning around the crowded room, this proud father happened to fix on the gaze of his wife's eyes upon him and as their eyes met, they locked in mutual understanding. God had been good to this family during the years that had scrolled by and there was so much to be grateful for.

Perhaps there had never been a more doting grandfather than James. And perhaps there had never been a grandfather more aware of the wonderful responsibility he carried, to leave a Godly inheritance for his children and their children in turn.

The experience in the attic that James liked to refer to as his "upper room encounter" had shaped this man's life profoundly. It had proved to be a defining moment and it profoundly influenced his life and every choice he made thereafter. James accorded that experience as being the moment when he recognized something evil and cloying had been released from the Pollock family line…it was as if he had stood up to claim a *new* inheritance and he had continued to confidently live in the expectation of his family's new destiny. The old negative patterns and traits apparent in the Pollock family line had indeed been severed from that moment forward.

Now he sat proudly with his wife of fifty years, being honored on the occasion of their golden wedding anniversary. Surrounded by family, friends and some long-term colleagues from his days in the medical profession, James and Hannah were filled with gratitude for the honor being shown them on this day. They deserved this honor being bestowed upon them in the light of the kind, loving and attentive nurturing this couple had poured into their children and grandchildren.

Since his upper room encounter as a searching nineteen-year-old, James had determined to steadfastly walk in the "Presence" of the One he'd come to love and know more intimately each day. Through the harrowing wartime experiences and the circumstances under which he had ended up in Brockenhurst, England and meeting Hannah, James could see the sustaining hand of God at work in his life.

Unbeknown to Hannah, James sought her father's permission to wed his daughter and together they had planned for her family to come to New Zealand with a view to staying on after a grand wedding. When all the plans were in place, James attended in style to the formality of proposing to Hannah…a proposal she jubilantly accepted. Marrying her shortly after she and her family had arrived in New Zealand, James sought from the outset to fulfill his role as a husband, father and then later as a grandfather, drawing his life and example from Jesus.

As couple, they knew they never walked alone.

Of course there had been seasons of pain and hardships to walk through on occasion but an under-girding truth had held James and Hannah together. They shared an unshakeable strength that comes from faith in One who is perfect strength, whose promises for good and for blessing endure from generation to generation for those who trust Him. The knowledge that they would be leaving an enduring legacy of loving unity and fruitfulness for their family… a legacy of eternal value was sure and certain.

AUTHOR'S NOTE:

This book may have come to an end however for some readers, the "story" will be ongoing. I would respectfully suggest that you read my notes that follow as a conclusion to this book. This is my summary of the central theme of the story and it supplies to a significant degree, my motivation in creating the narrative. My notes express the essential message that total freedom in every area of our personality is possible. There is hope and there can be release from any form of bondage or hindrance in our lives regardless of where the source of the difficulty originates—whether it is of a generational nature or something else. I have also offered the titles of a couple of books I highly recommend that could provide valuable further reading and help.

A MESSAGE FROM THE AUTHOR

It used to bother me that in what is probably the most powerful encounter a human being living on planet earth has ever had with God, there appears to be a contradiction.

In Exodus Chapters 33 and 34, the instance is recorded when God spoke to Moses *face to face as a man speaks with his friend.*

"I beseech you," Moses cries out to God with deep longings and passion in his heart during this remarkable encounter, "S*how me your glory."*

Partly in response to Moses' desire for God, the Lord descends in cloud and proceeds to proclaim His Name to this amazing man… What follows is God's self portrait—a declaration of the attributes of the kindness and goodness that are an intrinsic part of who He is…

It is a description of His very nature. (Exodus 34: 6-7)

"The Lord God, merciful and gracious, long-suffering, and abundant in goodness and truth. Keeping mercy for thousands, forgiving iniquity, transgression and sin and that will by no means clear the guilty..."

The troublesome part is what comes next and it is this that could be seen to be at variance with who God has just declared Himself to be…

"...visiting the iniquity of the fathers upon the children and upon the children's children unto the third and to the fourth generation"

It sounds horribly vindictive doesn't it? Yet only if it is read in a way which communicates that God simply cannot wait to punish and '*get*' those who follow on in a family line for what their parents, grandparents and great grandparents did and that future children will face God's judgment because of the iniquity (generational sins, failures and brokenness) of their forebears. How would it be fair and how could it correlate with a God who has just stated His goodness and long suffering nature to punish a person for their forefather's failures?

I have come to understand that this is not what God is expressing and there is no contradiction here that needs reconciling. In fact what God is expressing here is the *principle of inheritance*. That is what this book is about.

When a person allows a door to open in their life through some sin, disorder or circumstance, an impact (depending on the magnitude of the incident), can occur whereby a spiritual *dynamic* becomes embedded in that person with inherent potential existing then for it to transfer on to their progeny.

We all recognize how physical hereditary factors transfer when a family member carries a clear resemblance to a parent or grandparent, build, facial similarity, hair or color of eyes and so on. We've heard sayings such as *"like father like son"* or *"he's a chip off the old block,"* referring to the physical or even the personality likenesses a son may carry from his father. But few people stop to consider that this same principle of inheritance, operating in a family line in a physical sense, operates *also* in the spiritual and soulish realm. This is important because we all carry inheritance that we will be passing on. It can be for good, but it can be for evil.

God was not saying in the Exodus passage that because your grandfather did this or had this experience, that you will now bear judgment for it and pay because I'm out to get you for wrongs or difficulties he got into. What is being stated is that there is a generational transfer of iniquity which flows down a family line and that where a door somehow got opened back down the line, the consequences are likely to reside and continue on from one generation to the next.

This is the sense in which the "sins of the fathers are visited upon the children."

Sometimes it is possible to observe this transfer of generational iniquity when a re-current "theme" or afflicting problem besets a family. There can be any number of issues—in this book the central character is impacted dreadfully by his father's inadequacies and infidelity. As a victim and recipient of that breach, he carries on himself to become a perpetrator of similar dysfunction in turn with his own family, perpetuating the inheritance of marriage failures in the line. Numerous other situations could be cited. Take for example evidence in a person's life of an addictive tendency, say perhaps alcoholism. Most often by going through the family line it can be observed that one here, another there throughout the line struggled with addiction of some sort. The nature of the addiction is not the issue—whether enslavement to alcohol, gambling, drugs, sexual perversity, violence, anger, an eating disorder or some other form of compulsive behavior. The point is, that vulnerability in the area of *addictiveness* has a hold in that generational line. It is remarkable to see that where such an *effect* is apparent, that it will usually (certainly not invariably), stem or originate from a *cause* and often that root cause is sourced where a door was opened by ancestral activity in the problem area that is potentially then visited upon the offspring.

Unfair? Well it's no more "unfair" than inheriting brown eyes or some physical attribute…it's the way we were designed—to pass on an inheritance and remember God's heart has **always** been for the succession to be for good—NOT evil!

An important issue to note is that the enemy of our soul has always looked for opportunity to gain a foothold or point of entry to exploit (see Ephesians 4:27)—Satan and his forces of darkness look for a 'place' of legal jurisdiction and will seize on any opening in an individual's life caused by sin, or even trauma and tragedy and see to it that wherever possible the negative trait is perpetuated and propelled as a stronghold in a family. It is interesting to note that only Jesus who was sinless, could say *"the prince of this world has come but he has no claim on Me—he has nothing in common with Me, there is nothing in Me that belongs to him, he has no power over Me."*

John 14:30 (Amplified Version)

The fact some families have a propensity to a weakness or certain trait (sometimes referred to as an "Achilles heel") is evidence of generational influence or heredity operating negatively. One could say such a trait may appear in many families of the general populace but the point is that when the incidence rate is observably higher in a particular family, sadly it is more likely than not, a case of something being visited on that family.

There are many ways a door can be opened and initiate things that in turn are passed on. It may be through acts of sinfulness or rebellion, it may even be through exposure to a terrible calamity or trauma which releases negative emotions such as *fear, shock, grief, insecurity, rejection, shame*. Such things readily become an entrenched, perpetuating legacy.

That is, until someone recognizing what is happening stands up in the family line and says *"enough"!* The good news is, that this dynamic (call it a curse if you will) needn't be accepted with any sort of resignation. *We* can and should leave a rich positive inheritance of blessing for successive generations in our family line. There can be release and a breaking of bondages that are generational.

There is a way out. That is what "salvation" (*sozo*—Greek, *wholeness*) offers, and Jesus died shedding His blood to take every sin, every curse, all shame upon Himself on the cross, so we can be truly free. In fact He offers us on the basis of His resurrection power, a totally *brand new inheritance*.

No wonder Paul the apostle declared confidently that anyone in Christ is a *"brand new creature and that old things have passed away and all things have become new" (*2Corinthians 5:17)

Now while of course every blessing and provision is made available *propositionally* through the cross, it certainly doesn't mean that it just automatically becomes the possession and the experience of everyone.

I have known sincere Christians who grappled for years with personal issues and freedom seemed to elude them—until recognizing their problem's source had originated generationally and they understood how to enforce their release! Of course it was always available, but there's so often occasions where victory must be claimed and specifically appropriated through faith in Christ's work for us. An invitation is extended—the offer must be received. Severing of generational influences may need a simple prayer of renunciation. This sounds a big word but all it means to *renounce* something, is to literally *speak it off* your life. Again Paul refers to the freedom that comes from having "renounced the *hidden* things of darkness" (2Corinthians 4:2)

Introspectively going looking for stuff to renounce that may be hidden is unnecessary because the Holy Spirit is our teacher and will bring anything that may be relevant to our attention. Through repentance, by turning and forsaking every inheritance that is contrary to that which flows to us from the cross, we can cast off every strand of negative inheritance and enter freedom indeed.

It is my hope that the story I have written will graphically open up this truth in a refreshing way and encourage you to seek your own life-transforming encounter. My desire would be that your resolve and determination to live in the true freedom and inheritance that is offered to us all will have increased through the reading of this book.

"A good man leaves an inheritance to his children's children." Proverbs 13:22

Recommended Reading

"Christian Set Yourself Free"
by Graham Powell

"Blessing or Curse: You Can Choose"
by Derek Prince